EDDY ST AND THE EPIC HOLIDAY ADVENTURE

By **Simon Cherry**

Illustrated by **Francis Blake**

A ROTTEN HOLIDAY BECOMES EPIC

The noise that interrupted Eddy Stone's breakfast was like a cow falling off a wardrobe.

"What the—?"

Eddy thought he knew every strange sound in his gran's old seaside cottage – the hot-water tap that coughed like a cat with a furball, the fizzle of the dodgy light switch on the landing, the moaning wind that blew through the crack in his bedroom wall. But this was something new – a deep bellow and a heavy THUMP that rippled the milk in his cereal bowl and rattled the cups on the kitchen dresser as it rumbled from the floorboards to the rafters. He didn't know it yet, but that noise meant that nothing was ever going to be the same again for Eddy.

Or for the little lump of plaster on the kitchen ceiling.

For over three hundred years, the little lump of plaster had quietly hung around, while generations of people had gathered beneath it to laugh and to argue, to choke on stray fishbones, or to ask if there was any more custard. Dogs had snaffled scraps from unguarded plates, cats had chased mice between chair legs, and on one rainy Thursday afternoon a boy called Walter had removed all his clothes, painted himself green, and told his mother that when he grew up he was going to be a frog. In all that time, the little lump of plaster had done absolutely nothing.

But today was going to be different. Today, this was going to be the little lump of plaster that *could*.

Over the years, it had gradually loosened its grip on the boards above, until only a crust of paint and a smear of old cobweb were holding it in place. And this was its moment. With that mighty thump that had so surprised Eddy, the little lump of plaster broke free.

Down it tumbled.

Down towards excitement.

Down towards adventure.

Down towards Eddy Stone's head.

"Ouch!"

Eddy reached up to rub
the bump where something
had just…

"Urgh!"

The something landed in his
cereal, splashing milk onto a
picture of a galleon in the book
that he was reading.

"Oh, great."

What Eddy wanted for his breakfast was a delicious bowl of Choccy Puffs (with extra added vitamins). What Eddy now had for his breakfast was a not-so-delicious bowl of Choccy Puffs with extra added ceiling – a dirty great chunk of it, oozing flakes of paint and matted strands of spider's web. The milk had already turned a dingy, dodgy shade of grey.

The little lump of plaster's adventure was over. But if you had asked it whether that brief moment had been worth waiting for, what do you think it would have said?

It would have said nothing at all, of course. Because it was just a little lump of plaster.

This summer holiday is rubbish, Eddy thought. *Why did Mum and Dad have to send me here? I've only been in Tidemark Bay for four days and it's a total disaster. I mean, could it get any worse?*

The world took a second to come up with an answer to Eddy's question. And then half the plaster on the kitchen ceiling fell down.

Eddy peered through a cloud of dust at the bare beams and exposed floorboards overhead. And then, he heard the voice. A deep, stranger's voice, where no voice should be, singing about a-heaving and a-hauling where the south winds blow-oh! It wasn't a some*thing* that had made that great thump, Eddy realized. It was a some*one*.

Ever so slowly, and ever so quietly, Eddy crept upstairs. The singing was coming from the bathroom.

Ever so carefully, and ever so gently, Eddy pushed open the bathroom door. The someone was sitting in the bath – with no water, and no bubbles, but with a full set of clothes. Very unusual clothes.

Ever so "Oh my gosh!" and ever so "What the heck?" Eddy stood and stared. It was a pirate.

There was a pirate sitting in the bath.

"But. What? How? Wow!" Words came tumbling and jumbling out of Eddy's mouth – along with a fountain of half-chewed bits of Choccy Puffs.

The pirate took off his three-cornered hat and blew the bits of Choccy Puffs away. Then he scraped the bits of Choccy Puffs out of his tangled black beard, flicked the bits of Choccy Puffs off the gold braid on his green coat, picked the bits of Choccy Puffs out of the tops of his long black boots, and brushed the bits of Choccy Puffs from his red and white striped breeches.

"Are you really a pirate?" asked Eddy.

The pirate coughed a single Choccy Puff from his throat and spoke in the slow voice you might use if you were trying to explain long division to a particularly stupid goat.

"No," he said. "I'm a fairy princess! Swab me down with a bucket of bilge water, what does it look like?"

"Pirate," said Eddy.

"And now that's sorted," said the pirate, "I've got a question for you. How can anyone sleep in this metal bed? It's harder than a stale ship's biscuit."

"It's not a bed," said Eddy, "it's a bath."

"Stinky fish!" shouted the pirate, jumping up and banging his head on the sloping bathroom ceiling. "I swore that I'd never set foot – or any other bit of me – in one of those things. 'T'ain't natural."

He hopped over the side of the bath.

"Be careful where you put your feet," Eddy warned him, "the floorboards are a bit iffy."

But he was too late. The pirate's left boot hit the floor. The floorboard gave a soggy shrug and got out of the way. The boot carried on straight through, followed by the rest of the pirate's leg.

"Look out below!" shouted the pirate. "That wood is as rotten as last Christmas's kippers. How did you let it get so bad?"

Eddy perched on the side of the bath. "Not me. It's my gran's place. My mum and dad said they were far too busy at work to look after me all summer, so they packed me off here to get rid of  me. They said I'd have lots of fun and fresh sea air. Well that was a load of rubbish. There's no fun – not unless you count the local kids throwing sticks and apple cores at me. But Mum and Dad were right about the fresh sea air – there's masses of it blowing in through the missing windowpanes. My gran has let the cottage get into a

9

terrible state," explained Eddy, picking at a patch of rust on the bath. "I think the whole place is going to fall down soon."

"And this floor is making an early start," said the pirate, struggling to pull his leg out of the hole.

"Gran doesn't even notice how bad it is," said Eddy. "She doesn't notice anything these days. She's got really scatty. Last night she put gravy granules in my hot milk instead of cocoa. Sweet and meaty – urgh! I can still taste it. But even if she did notice how bad the house is, I don't see what she could do. Putting all this right would cost a fortune."

"A fortune!" the pirate yelled. "That must be why I'm here! To save this cottage!"

With an almighty heave, he freed his leg from the hole in the floor – and from his boot, which stayed behind, dangling down into the kitchen below. He toppled onto his back, legs in the air. A grubby big toe, sticking out of the end of a moth-eaten sock, wafted under Eddy's nose.

"I had a dream last night," the pirate continued, "and that dream told me that I would meet someone who had need of a fortune, then set out on a quest. And in

my dream I found a map. And not just any old map –
a treasure map!"

"Treasure?" said Eddy. "I like the sound of that!"

"And not just any old treasure map. Oh, no. A word
appeared in my dream, a word written across the sky in
letters of fire. And that word was a name. And that
name was…" The pirate leaned forward and said in a
long, low whisper, "…Grungeybeard! And I don't need
to tell you what that means."

"Well," said Eddy, "you could give me a clue."

"You can't mean you've never heard of the richest
pirate who ever was?"

"I've read loads of books about ships and pirates,"
said Eddy, "and I'm sure none of them ever mentioned
a Grungeybeard."

"Never mind your books. We are going to find his
buried treasure!"

"We!" said Eddy. "You mean – me?"

"I'll need a good cabin boy. Instead of having no fun
here, why don't you come and have buckets of fun with
me? Have you got the guts and the gumption for an
adventure? And if we're really lucky, maybe we'll get to
fire a massive cannon and explode a few things while

we're about it."

"Adventure! Treasure! Explosions! No more beefy cocoa! You bet!" said Eddy. Suddenly the summer holiday didn't seem so terrible after all. "Oh, but I suppose I'd better ask my gran first."

A DEAL IS STRUCK – AND SO IS EDDY

The pair padded downstairs. As the pirate hauled his dangling boot down from the hole in the kitchen ceiling, there was a cry of "Lovely plums!" from the front room.

"That's my gran," Eddy explained.

"If she's got plums in there I wouldn't say no," said the pirate. "I'm feeling peckish and a nice bit of fruit would go down a treat."

"It's not fruit," said Eddy. "It's her fruit machine. When I was little, she owned the biggest amusement arcade in Tidemark Bay. They called her the One-Armed Bandit Queen. But then people stopped coming to the arcade and she had to close it down. I think the strain of that was what made her go scatty. Now she's just got one machine in the front room. And there's a giant jar full of old ten-pence pieces that she feeds into it, and when she runs out she unlocks the machine and puts them back in the jar and starts again. She spends hours on it every day."

"The One-Armed Bandit Queen," the pirate repeated. "She sounds like quite a woman. But do you mean that she only had one arm and was the queen of a gang of bandits, or that she was the queen of a gang and the bandits in it only had one arm apiece?"

"No," said Eddy. "It wasn't like that. You pull a handle and…" He could tell from the way that the pirate was looking at him that he wasn't making any sense. "It's a bit hard to explain. But if you're hungry, there's some cold chicken in the fridge. I'll get it."

Eddy's gran had said he could help himself to anything he wanted, so he didn't think she'd mind if the chicken got eaten. In fact, he didn't think she would even notice if the chicken got eaten.

He lifted the bird out of the fridge – and jumped back in surprise.

"Yow!"

He hadn't expected to find a set of false teeth behind it. They grinned at him from the butter dish.

"You all right, lad?"

"I'm fine. It's just my gran mixing things up again. I suppose that explains why there was a slice of pork pie in a glass of water in the bathroom last night."

"I wondered about that," said the pirate. "It weren't much of a breakfast. That soak didn't improve the flavour."

Eddy handed him the chicken.

"I'd better take these teeth to Gran. And a couple of pickled onions. She loves them. I bet she has forgotten to eat anything this morning."

Eddy found his gran in the middle of a particularly tricky nudge to line up three oranges. He waited until she had finished before asking her, "Is it all right if I go off today for an adventure with a pirate?"

His gran was used to Eddy's imagination. Yesterday he had told her he was off to meet a spaceman and zap aliens on the beach. The day before he had gone to the woods with an explorer to find a lost jungle tribe.

"That's fine," she said, adjusting her teeth. "It's nice

that you've made so many imaginary friends. Just make sure you're back in time for tea. And don't lose your socks."

"Okay," said Eddy. "But he's not imaginary. He's real."

"Of course he is. And has this pirate of yours got a name?" She crunched a pickled onion.

"I don't know," said Eddy as he left the room, "I'll ask him."

⚓ ⚓ ⚓

"A name!" said the pirate, as they set off down the lane. "Course I got a name. I'm Mad Bad Jake McHake. But you can call me Captain."

"Are you really mad and bad?"

"Well, I get very grumpy if I accidentally button my beard into my trousers when I'm getting dressed. And what do they call you round here?"

"Round here they usually call me 'Oi! Cityboy Snotface!' Or just 'Oi!' for short. But at home my friends call me Eddy. Eddy Stone."

"Pleased to meet you," said the Captain.

As they approached a bend in the lane, two heads popped up from behind the hedge in front of them.

"Oi, Cityboy Snotface!" shouted the bigger boy.

"Oi!" added the smaller boy.

"I'd bet my boots they must mean you," the Captain said to Eddy.

They did.

There was a sudden blur of arms, and two squishy tomatoes hurtled towards Eddy.

Luckily, the first tomato missed him. But the second tomato was not so fortunate. It splatted onto his T-shirt in a mush of seeds.

The two boys howled with delight and ran off across the field.

Eddy pulled a tissue from his pocket and wiped the mess.

"I can't wait to get away from here," he said. "No one wants to be friends."

"You needs to stand up for yourself," said the Captain. "Show them they can't just walk all over you."

"The first time the local boys threw sticks at me," said Eddy, "I thought about throwing them back. But what's the point? They'd just go and get bigger sticks. And there are more of them than me. But I won't have to put up with it much longer. Not once we start our treasure hunt."

They walked down into the town. Tidemark Bay had

once been a busy holiday resort full of people eating fish and chips and getting so much sun that they had to go and lie down with the curtains closed in their hotel bedrooms. But these days, people preferred to get onto planes and go and eat fish and chips on foreign beaches and get so much sun that they had to lie down with the curtains closed in foreign hotel bedrooms. They thought this was much more exciting.

These days, Tidemark Bay looked as lonely and lost as a sheep in a supermarket.

"First thing we need," said the Captain, "is to find that treasure map."

"Great," said Eddy. "Where do we look?"

"In my dream there was an old junk shop with a window full of broken furniture and a big old machine that no one knew the use of. And it was owned by someone who had no idea what to charge for anything. And in the back of the shop, under a layer of dust and a glass case with a stuffed lobster dressed as a soldier and a copper jelly mould shaped like an octopus, there was a shabby old sailor's chest with a secret compartment with the treasure map inside."

They turned the corner. In front of them was an old

junk shop with a window full of three-legged chairs and a cupboard with no doors and a big old machine with sign on it that said: *Antique potato peeler?* It had a price ticket, on which the shop owner had written *£39.50* and then crossed it out and put *75 pence* and then crossed that out and put *18 Euros*.

"Aha!" said the Captain. "Follow me!" He stepped inside.

"Can I help you, dearie?" asked the grey-haired lady who owned the shop.

"Just having a snout about, thank'ee," answered the Captain.

A sudden gleam from the back of the shop caught their eye. A shaft of sunlight glinted off a copper jelly mould shaped like an octopus. The mould was standing on a glass case containing a stuffed lobster dressed as a soldier. And underneath, coated in a thick layer of dust, was what looked very like a shabby old sailor's chest.

"Leave this to me," whispered the Captain. "Shops like this charge you a fortune if they knows you're after a particular thing. You have to pretend that you really want to buy something else, and just mention that you might also be a little bit interested in, say, a shabby old sailor's chest. That way, you get a better price."

He turned to the shop owner, and noticed that the wall behind her was covered with paintings. Big, blobby, brightly coloured paintings.

"Good day, honest shopkeeper. That's a very nice painting." He pointed to a blazing yellow splodge, which was dotted with purple streaks.

"Really?" said the shop owner. She was rather surprised, because she knew it was in fact a dreadful painting. Like all the paintings in her shop, it was the work of her auntie, who had no artistic talent at all. A donkey holding a paintbrush between its teeth would have done better. While wearing a blindfold.

The shop owner only kept the paintings because she was too polite to hurt her auntie's feelings.

"Lovely picture of – um – a nice doggy," said the Captain.

"It's the Taj Mahal by moonlight, dearie," said the shop owner.

"I'll give you two doubloons for it," said the Captain.

"Forty pounds," bargained the shop owner, who hadn't a clue how much a doubloon was worth in modern money.

"Three doubloons," answered the Captain, who hadn't a clue either but wasn't going to give in.

"Thirty."

"Three doubloons and a ring with a picture of a mermaid on it."

"Sold!"

The Captain spat on his palm and shook the shop owner's hand to seal the deal.

WANTED ON VOYAGE

A rattle of coins and a mermaid ring later, the Captain and Eddy were out on the pavement clutching a remarkably lifelike painting of a giant blob of custard and jam.

"Now, that's what I call a bargain!" said the Captain.

"But not what you'd call a treasure map," Eddy pointed out. "Perhaps this time you should leave it to me."

They went back into the shop. The shop owner was wiping spit off her hand with a tea towel covered in pictures of jellyfish of the world.

"We're interested in that chest," said Eddy.

"Oh, yes," said the shop owner. "It used to belong to a shabby old sailor."

"Do you have any idea of its true value?"

"Not the slightest, dearie," said the shop owner.

"It's one pound thirty-two pence," said Eddy. Luckily, that was exactly how much he had in his pocket.

"It's a deal," said the shop owner, who was delighted to have sold two things in one day. "I'll just move the glass case with the lobster and the copper jelly mould so we can get it out. And then I suppose you'll want me to show you how to open the secret compartment with the treasure map inside?"

THE LEGEND OF GRUNGEYBEARD

"There's a knack to opening this chest," said the shop owner. "The shabby old sailor showed me. First you have to twist the dolphin's head that's carved on the front." As she turned her hand, a panel next to the dolphin's head slid back, revealing a crystal shaped like a teardrop.

"Then you have to move the chest into the sunlight."

Eddy and the Captain pushed the chest forward. As light hit the crystal teardrop, it began to glow pink, and a flap on the top of the chest suddenly flipped open. With a gentle whirring of clockwork and cogs, a tiny golden harp rose into view.

"Then you have to strum the harp."

She ran her hand across the strings. The notes crept into the shop like an angel's whisper, then swelled into a tune so beautiful it would have melted a wasp's heart. The crystal filled even the gloomiest corner of the shop with its pink glow, and the chest itself seemed to throb with a mysterious energy. Eddy felt the music flowing through him, tingling from his toes to his nose.

"And then," said the shop owner, "you do this."

She drew back her foot and kicked the chest as hard as she could. The glow vanished, the music fell silent, the chest let out a loud groan, and a hidden drawer shot across the shop like a missile. It bounced off a wicker basket, smashed a chunk out of a vase, clanged into an old bucket, and flipped over in the air.

Something faded and dusty fell to the floor, and unrolled towards them. Its edges were tattered. It was streaked and stained. It had a compass drawn in one corner, and islands with jagged mountains and palm trees, and at its top the words *A Treasure Map*. It lay before them, full of excitement and creases and a smell like old cabbage.

"A real pirate treasure map!" shouted Eddy.

"Grungeybeard!" shouted the Captain.

"Excuse me, dearie," said the shop owner, "but what is a grungeybeard?"

"Not you as well?" said the Captain. "Settle your bottoms and pin back your ears, and I will tell you a tale – a tale of greed and folly and cruelty and madness – for I will tell you The Tale of Grungeybeard the Pirate!"

"Could you do it without the funny voice, please?" asked Eddy.

"What funny voice?"

"That one – you've gone all strange and wobbly and old-fashioned."

"Have I? Sorry. Ahem. I mean, sorry. Right then – he was a wild one, was Grungeybeard. The terror of the high seas – him and his ship *The Primrose*. And you've got to be a real terror to get away with calling your ship after something as weedy as that. He thought it were a laugh to see grown men tremble when they heard the name of a little flower. But that was Grungeybeard for you – the only thing sharper than his sense of humour was his cutlass.

"For five fearless years he robbed and looted, and

gathered the greatest hoard of treasure that any pirate has ever seen. And he had a high old time. He loved his luxuries – fine wines, expensive chocolates, lobster and caviar for breakfast. And he loved being famous, too. He paid poets to write verses and spread the news of his latest daring deeds.

"But all that treasure started to weigh on his mind. And his mind couldn't bear it. If anyone admired the gold buttons on his waistcoat, or the silver buckles on his shoes, or the diamonds he'd had set in his teeth, Grungeybeard thought they meant to steal them. If anyone shook him by the hand, Grungeybeard would count the ruby rings on his fingers afterwards to check they were still all there. And then he'd count his fingers, to be doubly sure.

"So he decided to take all his most valuable treasure, and bury it in a secret place where no one would be able to find it. He loaded up a great oak

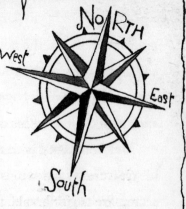

chest – they do say that there
were pearls as big as conkers,
diamonds as big as gulls' eggs,
and emeralds as big as very
fat hamsters.

"One moonlit night he took his two most trusted
crew members, rowed to a tropical island and
buried the chest. Then he decided that even his
most trusted crew members couldn't be trusted to
keep the secret of where they had hidden it. So he
shot them both. It is said that they died with a
terrible curse on their lips – a curse on
Grungeybeard and his riches.

"And then – nobody knows. There's some do say
he decided that he couldn't even trust himself
not to give away the secret by talking in his sleep,
so he shot himself, too. There's some do say he
went stark mad and had a great ship built out of
solid gold that slipped straight off the launching

ramp and down to the bottom of the sea – taking him and all his crew with it. And there's some do say he changed his name to Nigel, opened a small tea shop, and spent the rest of his days baking scones.

"And from that day to this, no one ever knew where his treasure lay hidden. Until this map gave up his secret. We're going to be rich, Eddy my lad. We sail with the tide!"

"Brilliant!" shouted Eddy. "I mean, aye aye Captain! Where do we meet the rest of your crew?"

"Stinky fish!" shouted the Captain. "I knew I'd forgotten something. We needs a crew."

The shop owner coughed quietly.

"Ahem! I'd love to sail with you."

"You?" said the Captain, looking her up and down. The shop owner blinked up at him through her spectacles. "Have you ever been to sea?"

"I took the ferry to France once."

"Can you handle a cutlass in the heat of battle?"

"I'm sure I'd pick it up. I'm a dab hand with a potato peeler."

"This is a voyage of peril and endeavour. I'd have to be desperate to sail with you on board."

"Oh," said the shop owner, trying very hard not to sound disappointed.

"What I needs," said the Captain, "is a gang of salt-seasoned old sea-dogs, with sailing in their sinews and spirit in their stomachs. Now where in all the wide blue yonder am I going to find them?"

EVERYTHING A PIRATE CAPTAIN COULD NEED

"I've read about this," said Eddy. "Pirate captains hire their crews in rough old backstreet inns full of black-hearted villains who'd sell their own grannies for ninepence."

"Quite right," said the Captain. "Let's go and hunt round town."

They soon found a damp and dingy alley leading to a damper and dingier courtyard. A rat scuttled away through a hole into the dirtiest, grottiest, smelliest and stickiest building that Eddy had ever seen. In fact, it was so dirty, grotty, smelly and sticky that a moment later the rat staggered out again, coughing and gasping for air.

A grimy sign swung above their heads – *The Tidemark Bay Rough Tough Club.*

Eddy spotted a blotchy handwritten note pinned to the door.

"Look, Captain. 'Grannies for sale. Various sizes. Enquire within.'"

"Perfect," said the Captain.

But it wasn't perfect. It was shut.

Eddy saw another notice in the window, where it had been stuck with the remains of a meat and potato pie.

"It says, 'Away on our Shout Round Europe summer coach trip. See you softies in two weeks.'"

"We can't wait that long," said the Captain. "We needs to catch the tide. This is desperate."

"Desperate? Then I'm your woman," said the shop owner, popping out from behind an old barrel. "Please, Captain. You can't imagine what it's like to stand in that shop week after week. Some days I don't see a single soul. I've always dreamed of sailing off on an adventure. Give me a chance, dearie."

The Captain sighed. "I don't seem to have a choice. Oh, well. From now on, you will be known as the Crew.

You will call me Captain, and I will call you anything I like, because I'm in charge. Is that clear?"

"Yes, dearie," said the Crew.

"You call me Captain."

"Yes, Captain, dearie."

"Now, before we set sail we will need some essential kit. Like a telescope."

"Got one!" said the Crew. She dragged an enormous red rucksack from behind the barrel, rummaged around, and pulled out a brass telescope.

"And a compass."

"Got one!"

"And a…"

"Log book, hammock, lantern, inkstand, quill pen and barrel of rum. Got them."

"Gosh," said Eddy. "Everything but the—"

"Kitchen sink," interrupted the Crew. "Got one. All that a pirate captain could need."

"Then where's my carrot?" asked the Captain. "To sit on my shoulder."

"Don't you mean parrot?" asked Eddy.

"Carrot," said the Captain.

"My books say that pirates had parrots on their shoulders."

"Your books hadn't even heard of Grungeybeard," said the Captain. "I bet they were written by a load of landlubbers who don't know what they're talking about. One day one of them puts parrot instead of carrot by mistake and before you know it they're all copying it. I ask you, who'd want a parrot on his shoulder? It would be forever pecking your earhole and pooing down the back of your coat. Daft idea."

"And why do you want a carrot?" asked Eddy.

"The sea holds many secrets," said the Captain. "And that is one of them."

They found a greengrocer's shop round the corner. Outside it stood a large sack of carrots. The Captain began to pick through them, and soon spotted a

medium-sized one with a slightly
wonky end.

"This one's for me," he said.
"A carrot with character." He perched it on his right
shoulder. The carrot fell off.

"He just needs to find his sea legs," said the Captain.

"But we're not at sea," said Eddy.

"Well there you are then," answered the Captain.
"How could he possibly have found his sea legs when
we're still ashore? And now it's time we weren't ashore
no more. The waves wait for no man."

"The harbour's this way," said Eddy. "Let's board
your ship."

"My ship? Rudders and rigging!" shouted the
Captain. "I knew there was something else I'd forgotten.
Come on – there must be a spare one down there!"

"You can't just take someone's ship," said Eddy.
"That's stealing."

"It's not stealing," said the Captain. "It's borrowing.
It's what pirates do. It's amazing what people will lend
you after you wave your sword around and shout a bit."

He broke into a trot. But with his big boots flopping
and his long coat flapping and his scabbard getting

tangled with his legs, he couldn't run very fast. And every few strides the ship's carrot fell off his shoulder and he had to stop to pick it up. So even though Eddy had the yellow painting rolled up under his arm and was dragging the sailor's chest behind him, and even though the Crew was hauling her enormous red rucksack around, they all reached the harbour together.

"Jellyfish juice," muttered the Captain. "Where is everybody?"

⚓ ⚓ ⚓

Twenty years ago, the harbour had been the busiest part of a bustling fishing village. You couldn't move for boats coming in and out, crates of fish being unloaded, and salty old sailors mending their nets.

Ten years ago, the harbour had been the busiest part of a lively holiday resort. You couldn't move for visitors taking a boat trip, or buying fish and chips, or visiting the town museum to see a couple of actors pretending to be salty old sailors mending their nets.

Now the fishermen had retired, and the holidaymakers had stopped coming. The harbour was still the busiest place in town. But even the busiest place in Tidemark Bay was almost deserted. By a pile of tattered old fishing nets, two seagulls were squabbling noisily over the crumbs from a packet of prawn cocktail flavoured crisps.

The harbour was empty – apart from a lonely rowing boat that bobbed on the tide.

"Will that do, dearie Captain?" asked the Crew.

"Will it do?" said the Captain. "We're off to sail the seven seas, not to paddle around a puddle. Course it won't do."

Eddy's face fell. "We can't get anywhere without a ship," he said.

The Captain turned to look at him.

"Hang on a minute," said the Captain. "What's this, then?"

Behind Eddy stood a large wooden shed that had been decorated to look like an old sailing ship. The walls were curved like a hull, with a pointed prow at one end. The flat roof had low wooden railings running round it, like a deck. A plastic cannon poked through and pointed out over the harbour. A ship's wheel stood by a flagpole that was painted to look like a mast. Above the remains of some ragged cotton sails a flag fluttered limply in the breeze. The flag bore the faded words

Captain Cockle's Crunchy Cod Cakes.

It was a snack bar. Or rather, it had been a snack bar. Captain Cockle had sold his last crunchy cod cake long ago. The place was closed down and boarded up.

"Come on," shouted the Captain. He scrambled up a rope ladder that was hanging from the roof, then hauled Eddy and the Crew up after him.

He looked around with a grin.

"Say hello to our new vessel."

"We can't sail off in this," said Eddy.

"Why not?" asked the Captain. "You can't call this stealing. Look at the state of it. It's obvious that no one else wants it."

"We still can't sail off in it."

"We'll bring it back."

"But we still can't sail off in it."

"Why not?"

"It's a shed. You can't set sail in a shed."

"Never mind that," said the Captain. He reached into his coat pocket and pulled out a black flag with a skull and crossbones on it. "You haul down that tattered old flag and put this up in its place. Crew!"

"Yes, dearie."

"You mean, 'Aye aye, Captain'."

"That's right, dearie."

"Cast off and set a course for the high seas."

"Aye aye, Captain dearie! And by the way…" She tucked the carrot under the gold braid on the shoulder of the Captain's coat. "There, now. That should stop it falling off any more."

"This is nuts," Eddy muttered to himself. He unknotted the rope on the flagpole and pulled down the old Captain Cockle flag. So much for adventure. He'd been really excited. Never mind that his parents didn't want him around, or that his gran kept losing the plot, or that the local kids were horrible to him. He was going to forget all of that because he was off to find buried treasure and to save his gran's cottage from falling down. But now, without a ship, it was just another game – and a stupid one. He could have sat on a shed roof and pretended to be a pirate on his own if he'd wanted to. It had turned into a big disappointment – like being offered a huge box of chocolates and then finding out that every one of them was a lime cream. He hated lime creams.

Just as he finished tying the rope to the skull and crossbones flag, the planks beneath his feet suddenly lurched, almost knocking him over. When he looked up, there was no sign of the harbour.

All he could see around him was a great expanse of blue-green water.

He was standing on the deck of a ship. It wasn't very big, and it was all a bit tatty – the deck was worn and splintered, the rigging was frayed, and the sails that flapped in the wind had been yellowed and gnawed by the weather. But it was definitely a ship. And it was at sea.

SUN, SEA AND SICK

"That's more like it!" shouted the Captain. "Crew!"

"Aye aye, Captain, dearie!"

"Unfurl the mizzen mid-gallant, haul in the for'ard bleachers, make fast the jib-cleats, double-up the yardarm stays and hold a course nineteen degrees north-north-west – there's a hard blow rising to larboard that'll shake the teeth from our heads if we don't face her down!

"Well," added the Captain, "what are you waiting for?"

"Sorry, dearie," said the Crew, "but would you mind saying that again – a bit more slowly?"

The Captain took a deep breath.

"Is there summat wrong with your ears?" he asked. "I said, unfurl the mizzen mid-gallant, haul in the for'ard—"

"Yes, yes," the Crew interrupted, "but would you mind saying that again a bit more slowly – and in English?"

"I said, unfurl the… Oh for goodness' sake, steer straight ahead and try not to bump into any big rocks."

"That's better, dearie," said the Crew, taking the ship's wheel.

"I don't understand," Eddy said to the Captain. "One minute we were on the roof of a shed, and the next it had turned into this ship."

"Never underestimate the power of a treasure map," said the Captain. "There's something out there as wants to be found, and won't let the lack of a ship get in the way. Welcome aboard the good ship *Codcake*."

"Where are we? This isn't Tidemark Bay."

"Unless I'm very much mistaken, that place behind us," the Captain pointed towards a distant coastline, "is my home village of Pirate Cove. And I'm not very much mistaken, because that *is* Pirate Cove, and behind us is a very good place for it to be. And this big bluey-green wet thing all round us is what sailors call – the sea."

Eddy had seen the sea at Tidemark Bay in all weathers, but he had never seen it this colour. *It's as blue as a peacock's feather and as green as a gooseberry*, he thought. *No, it's as blue as a sapphire and as green as an emerald. No, it's as blue as a summer sky and as green as the Crew's face.*

The Crew was not looking well. The rolling, rocking, lurching, listing, swooping and swelling motion of the ship was all too much.

The Crew was seasick.

"This is the life, eh? You can be anyone you want to be out here and there's no one to tell you you can't," said the Captain. He slapped the Crew on the back.

"Please don't do that, dearie," said the Crew, in a quiet, clammy voice.

"Feeling a bit green about the gunwales, are we?" said the Captain. "Happens to the best of them on their first voyage. I bet I know how you're feeling – like your skin has turned to cold rice pudding."

"Do stop," whimpered the Crew.

"And your legs have gone loopy, and your guts are like a sackful of fox cubs who have drunk too much lemonade. And you think everything would be all right if you could just be sick. But you can't."

"I might," said the Crew.

"Every sailor knows that feeling," said the Captain. "And some of them sing about it."

He pulled a concertina from his coat pocket, and began a rousing rackety sea shanty.

"What shall we do with the seasick sailor
What shall we do with the seasick sailor
What shall we do with the seasick sailor
Early in the morning?

HUEY! And up it rises
GROOEY! And up it rises
SPEWEY! And up it rises
Early in the morning."

By the second verse, the green colour had spread from the Crew's cheeks to the tips of her ears.

"If he's feeling queasy and he needs to retch up
Feed him something greasy that he's sure to fetch up
Sausage, egg and bacon <u>and</u> a pint of ketchup
Early in the morning."

"This isn't helping very much," the Crew said. "Oh. Yes it is," she added a moment later, and ran to lean over the side of the ship.

When she turned round, she was looking a lot less green and a lot more perky.

"Right," said the Captain, "that's quite enough singing for one morning. There's work for us Codcakers to do. Helmsman! That's you," he said, throwing the Crew a length of rope. "Tie the wheel in place to keep us on course."

"Aye aye, dearie," replied the Crew enthusiastically.

"Deckhand! That's also you – find a mop and swab the decks."

"Aye aye, dearie," replied the Crew slightly less enthusiastically.

"Lookout—"

"Let me guess who that is," said the Crew.

"Climb up to the crow's nest and see what you can spot."

"I'm a Crew, not a crow, dearie," muttered the Crew.

"And no more muttering in the ranks. Any more muttering and I'll tell the cook to reduce your rations. Which reminds me – Cook! What's for lunch?"

"What supplies have we got, dearie?" asked the Crew.

"How should I know?" replied the Captain. "You're the cook, get the cabin boy to go below decks and see what's in the hold."

"And I suppose I must be the cabin boy, too," said the Crew.

"Don't be ridiculous," said the Captain. "You're far too old to be the cabin boy. Eddy is the cabin boy. Eddy! Are you ready for some orders?"

"You bet!" said Eddy. "Following a real pirate captain on a hunt for treasure – this is so much better than playing on my own back in Tidemark Bay."

"Take this lantern down below and see what you can find to eat. Oh, and watch out for rats. I've never known a ship yet that didn't have a few of them sharp-toothed little varmints lurking in the hold. You be careful down there."

WHAT LURKS IN THE SHADOWS?

The air below deck smelled of salt and tar. *The Codcake's* timbers creaked and groaned as Eddy held a lantern high above his head to light his way. The hold was stacked with crates and trunks and sacks filled with all sorts of things that would be useful on a voyage. There were ropes and candles and hammers and nails and dishes and forks and boots and spades and axes and saws and cups and spoons and saucepans and buckets and needles and cloth and absolutely nothing to eat.

Eddy searched into the farthest corners. What did his books say that old ships carried for long voyages?

Dry biscuits and barrels of salt beef and pickled herrings and mouldy cheese full of maggots. That's what he was looking for.

Well, maybe not the cheese.

In the light from his lantern, the piles of supplies cast long shadows across the wooden walls. A sudden ocean swell set the lantern swinging, and the shadows stretched and strayed like living creatures.

This is creepy, thought Eddy. *But it's just a trick of the light. Nothing to worry about. And if I keep thinking that, it will probably turn out to be true.*

Wait a minute. Hadn't that one shadow on the far side just moved in the opposite direction to all the others?

Eddy froze.

And then he heard it – a scratching, pattering, shuffling sound coming from behind a pile of crates to his right.

It must be rats! Just like the Captain had warned him.

He looked around for a weapon. There was a pile of shovels to his left. He quietly picked one up. That would do. Holding it in his right hand, with the lantern in his left, he crept towards where the sound was coming from.

He was almost on top of it now. Just behind this big crate. He put his lantern down on the floor, took hold of the shovel with both hands, and peeped round the corner. Ahead of him, in the gloom, a shape was scuttling around. A big shape.

Rats, Eddy knew, could be vicious. And one as big as this... Its teeth must be – no, he really didn't want to think about its teeth. Fighting it might not be a good idea. Trying to frighten it off was a much better plan. But could he scare it more than it scared him?

He took a deep breath and silently counted down: *Three...two...one...*

As he reached zero, he gripped the shovel tight and jumped out, yelling at the top of his voice.

"AAAAARRRRGGGHHHHHH!"

"AAAAARRRRGGGHHHHHH!"

the rat shouted back, rooted to the spot.

It was a funny-looking rat, thought Eddy, still shouting. For a start, it had a big, white tummy. Which he could see because it was standing up on its hind feet. Which were wide and yellow. And its fur didn't look quite right. A bit fluffy. And there was definitely something stumpy about its front legs. And it seemed to be wearing a false nose – a long, pointed, yellow false nose. Which was open. And shouting.

"AAAAARRRR-GGGHHHHH!"

Eddy stopped shouting as suddenly as he had started.

"You're not a rat," he said.

"Oh, well done," said the not-a-rat. "Top marks. I'll give you a clue. I'm not a zebra, either. Or a panda. Or a giant humbug. And you are not a fish. More's the pity."

"You're a penguin."

"Ten out of ten. Big gold star. What on earth are you doing going round yelling and frightening me like that?"

"You frightened me first."

"Oh, of course. Pardon me. There I was, quietly toddling round, minding my own business. Yes, I can see how that would be absolutely terrifying."

"I'm sorry if I frightened you. I heard noises. I got a bit jumpy. A lot has been happening today. It's very strange. In fact, come to think of it, it's about as strange as standing here chatting to a penguin. I didn't know penguins could talk."

"Have you ever asked one?"

"What are you doing down here anyway?" said Eddy, ignoring the question.

The Penguin leaned forward and whispered, "I'm on the run from the ocean theme park just up the coast. I was one of the performers in the big show – *Fishy Frolics*

– three times daily. I had to get out. There's only so many times you can slide down a ramp on your stomach to catch a herring before you start to lose your dignity."

"It sounds terrible," agreed Eddy.

"Terrible?" said the Penguin. "It was torture. Stuck in the chorus line. Me! I can do the comedy dancing, I said. I can play the tunes on the motor horns better than that stupid sealion. Give me a break, I said, I'll show you. I was born to be a star. But would they listen? Would they flip. So I ran away – to find my own spotlight. I've been in here working on a new act."

"Can I see it?" asked Eddy.

"If you throw me a fish," said the Penguin.

"I haven't got a fish," said Eddy.

"Well then," said the Penguin, "question answered."

"I think," said Eddy, "that I'd better take you to see the Captain."

LEARNING THE ROPES

"Blimey!" The Captain looked up from the treasure map that lay rolled out in front of him on the deck. "I saw a picture of one of those once. It's a funny sort of duck. A pinwing."

"That's penguin," said the Penguin. "And I'm not a duck."

"He was hiding down below," said Eddy, "and—"

"Hiding?" the Captain butted in. "Then he's a stowaway!"

"What's a stowaway?" asked the Penguin.

"Someone who thinks he can lie low and sneak a free ride. And the only thing to do with a stowaway like you is to put you ashore on the next uninhabited island we pass. Marooned. Alone for the rest of your life, with only the trees to talk to. After a few years you start to hear the trees talking back. You slowly go gibbering, blibbering, babbling bonkers. It's a fate worse than death. Until you eventually die – and then it's a fate that *is* death."

"Then I'm definitely not a stowaway," said the Penguin.

"So you must be a volunteer, ready to share the work," smiled the Captain. "Welcome aboard, Able Seaman Pinwing. You can start by polishing the anchor, darning the mainsail and tightening all the knots in the rigging."

"That sounds like a lot of work for one pair of flippers," said the Penguin. "Stowaway or volunteer – is that it? Aren't you forgetting the important position of ship's entertainer? Listen – here's one. What did the Atlantic Ocean say to the Pacific Ocean? Nothing – it just waved."

"Like I said. Stowaway or volunteer – which is it to be?" asked the Captain.

"Hold on," said the Penguin, "I need to think about this."

"You need to think about choosing between a bit of work and a horrible punishment?" asked the Crew.

"I'm not cut out for ordinary work," complained the Penguin. "There's show business in my blood and stardust in my eyes. My name should be up in lights."

"We're off on an adventure," said Eddy. "We're searching for treasure. You could be part of our story – and find fame and fortune."

"Fame? My number one favourite thing. Now you're talking," said the Penguin. "And fortune? My other number one favourite. Okay, I'm in. I volunteer."

"Then, for the second time," said the Captain, "welcome aboard, Able Seaman Pinwing!"

"But we need to sort out my part," said the Penguin. "All this able seaman do this, able seaman do that – it's just not me."

"So you're more a not-very-able seaman?" suggested the Crew.

"That suits me fine," said the Penguin. "By the way, Captain, do you know you've got a carrot on your shoulder?"

"Able or not, there's jobs to be done," said the Captain. "If we're going to find this treasure, we'll need to navigate. The ship's compass can tell us what direction we're going. But we needs to know how fast as well."

"I've read about how to do that," said Eddy. "You use a long rope with knots in it. You let it out as you travel, and you count how many knots go past in five minutes. Then it just takes a simple bit of maths to work out your speed."

"I've seen one of those over there," said the Crew, pointing across the deck to where the ship's rowing boat was lashed to a stout wooden post. A thick coil of rope was looped round the timber. "I wondered what it was for."

"Right," said the Captain, "Crew and Not Very Able Seaman Pinwing, get that rope over the side of the ship. And look lively!"

The Crew heaved and puffed, and the Penguin lent a reluctant flipper to the job.

The Captain turned back to his chart.

"What next, Captain?" asked the Crew.

"Now," said the Captain, "let out the rope as we travel."

"What rope?" asked the Crew.

"That rope that you just –" said the Captain, turning to face her – "hang on, what have you done with it?"

"Thrown it over the side, dearie," answered the Crew. "Following your orders."

"You're only supposed to throw the *end* into the water," shouted the Captain, "not the whole thing."

"You didn't say that, dearie."

"I can see this trip is going to be a long haul," said the Captain. "And now, how do you suppose we are going to work out where we are?"

"I think I know how," answered Eddy. "Look at this!"

He pointed to the map. In the top corner there was a small drawing of a ship. As they watched, it moved very slightly and very slowly.

"The map is showing us where we are," said Eddy. "It's like magic."

"Well, I'll be jiggered!" exclaimed the Captain. "If that's us, we should just be able to see that island."

He pointed to the map. Close to the tiny ship was a drawing of a small island, dotted with flowers and trees.

The Captain picked up his telescope, strode across *The Codcake*'s deck, and scanned the sea around them.

"Yes," he said. "Land ahoy! Just like on the map... wait a minute."

"What is it?" asked Eddy.

"It looks like we are not alone," said the Captain. "Over there. Coming up behind us on the starboard quarter. See what you make of it. Your eyes are probably sharper than mine."

He handed the telescope to Eddy. Sure enough, there was another ship out on the water.

And it was heading towards them.

As it drew nearer, it became clearer.

"It's flying the Jolly Roger," said Eddy.

"Pirates!" said the Crew.

"How does that work?" asked the Penguin. "We're pirates. They are pirates. Is it all one big happy pirate family?"

"Depends," said the Captain, "on who they are."

"I can just make out the letters on the front of the ship," said Eddy. "It's called the S – C – A – V – E – N – G – E – R. That spells…"

"Scavenger," said the Crew.

"No," said the Captain. "That spells trouble. Serious trouble."

8

THE MOST TERRIFYING SOUND IN <u>ALL</u> THE OCEAN

The Captain turned pale. The blood ran from his face. Then it hurried down his back, scurried down his legs and hid in his boots. He staggered slightly and grabbed hold of the mast for support.

"This is terrible," he said. "Of all the ships in all the world, we have to run into *The Scavenger*."

"Why is that so bad?" asked Eddy. The expression on the Captain's face made him wonder if he really wanted to hear the answer.

"It belongs to Barracuda Bill."

"I've seen a picture of a barracuda in a book about fish," said Eddy. "It's big and very fierce, with a really ugly pointy head and lots of long, sharp teeth. So do they call him Barracuda Bill because he's big and very fierce, too?"

"No, they call him Barracuda Bill because he's got a really ugly pointy head and lots of long, sharp teeth. But he is big and really fierce, as well. And he's feared the length and breadth of the ocean. He'll stop at nothing and nothing will stop him. And he's heading straight for us."

"Can we get away?" said Eddy. "Can we outrun him?"

"To go faster than him," said the Captain, "we'd need to hoist more sails than him. To hoist more sails than him, we'd need more crew than him. He's got a hundred hardened pirates, and we've got a boy, a lady who runs a shop and a pinwing. Can you see where this is going?"

There was no doubt that *The Scavenger* was closing in on them. And the closer it got, the larger it looked. And the larger it looked, the scarier it became.

Eddy could just hear the voices of *The Scavenger*'s crew, chanting in rhythm. Between each line they stamped twice on the deck with their boots – BOOM BOOM – and the sound carried across the waves like an enormous drum.

**"BOOM
BOOM**
What we doing?
**BOOM
BOOM**
Where we going?
**BOOM
BOOM**
Are we there yet?"

"The most terrifying sound in all the ocean," said the Captain. "That song means only one thing – fighting and stealing and burning and yelling and hitting and hurting and bashing and robbing and smashing and looting and sheer misery."

The Scavenger was soon close enough for Eddy to be able to see the owners of the voices – and what a wild and beardy and brutal bunch they looked. The wildest and beardiest and most brutal-looking one of all let out a snarl, revealing a mouthful of long, sharp teeth.

"That's him," whispered the Captain. "That's Barracuda Bill."

Barracuda Bill waved his cutlass in the air.

"Take aim!" he shouted – and took two steps to his left.

Eddy realized with horror that Barracuda Bill had been standing right in front of a cannon. The Codcakers were now staring straight down its barrel.

"Fire!" Barracuda Bill's cutlass slashed the air. One of the pirates put a glowing taper to the fuse on the cannon. With a fizz of flame, a deafening BANG, and a cloud of smoke, a cannonball whistled towards *The Codcake*.

Oh, no! thought Eddy. At least, that's what he started to think, but the cannonball came so fast that he had only just got as far as "oh" and was nowhere near "no" when there was another BANG. The cannonball blew apart and a shower of something white fluttered over the deck.

Still dizzy with shock, Eddy picked one of the white things up. It was a leaflet, with a message printed in elegant lettering:

Dear LOSERS,

We regret that due to our EXTREMELY busy
schedule, we will be unable to board, loot,
kidnap, burn or sink you today. We have
had a good look at your ship, and to be honest
it just isn't big enough to make it worth changing
our plans. So few hours in the day, so many
horrible deeds to be done.

We trust that you will NOT take this personally,
and can assure you that as soon as we find a
space in our diary, we will be happy to hunt
you down and do you over. In the meantime,
we hope you sleep uneasily in your beds.

   With WORST wishes,

Captain Barracuda Bill
and <u>all</u> the boys on the bad ship
SCAVENGER.

"Well," said the Crew, "he knows how
to write a very polite note, and nobody with manners
like that can be all… Oh really, that is too much!"

Eddy looked up. On the deck of *The Scavenger*, a hundred pirates had turned their backs on *The Codcake*. A hundred pirates had dropped their trousers. A hundred pirates had bent over and waggled their hairy bottoms in the direction of the Codcakers.

A hundred and ninety-nine bare cheeks now shone palely in the bright sunshine. (The odd one belonged to a pirate called Frankie Halftrousers, who had lost one of his buttocks in a swordfight years before. The ship's carpenter had made him a false one out of a block of seasoned oak, but it was too heavy for everyday wear so he kept it back for formal occasions.)

The Codcakers watched as *The Scavenger* pulled away into the distance, and listened as its terrible chant grew fainter…

"**BOOM BOOM** *What we doing?*
BOOM BOOM *Where we going?*
BOOM BOOM *Are we there yet?*"

…until it was too quiet to hear.

Calm returned to *The Codcake*. A few leaflets swirled across her deck in the sea breeze.

"Right," said the Captain. "Now, where were we?"

"We were looking at this," Eddy answered, leaning over the map again. As he watched, letters started to appear, writing themselves across its surface.

"Captain," he said. "You've got to see this! It's amazing!"

"Shiver my socks!" said the Captain. "I've never known a map like this before."

"Well," said the Crew, "I may run a junk shop, but I don't just sell any old rubbish, you know."

Eddy read out the message that had appeared:

<u>HERE BEGINS YOUR QUEST FOR TREASURE.</u>
YOU MUST COLLECT FOUR OBJECTS
TO PROVE YOU DESERVE TO WIN THE PRIZE.

<u>LEVEL ONE.</u> SAIL TO THE DESERTED ISLAND OF BLOSSOM AND FIND THE FIRST OBJECT, THE FABLED WARBLEFLOWER, WHICH GROWS ONLY AT THE TOP OF THE HIGHEST CLIFF. RETURN WITH THE FLOWER TO UNLOCK THE NEXT LEVEL. BUT BEWARE! THE WAY IS DIFFICULT, AND REQUIRES STRENGTH AND COURAGE.

"Grungeybeard's treasure, here we come," said the Captain.

"A flower?" said Eddy. "Why on earth would Grungeybeard want us to find a flower?"

"I reckon that's Grungeybeard's sense of humour through and through," said the Captain. "He'd have a right laugh thinking of us climbing a huge cliff just to pick a plant. We've got to meet the challenge and show we're worthy of the reward."

He drew his sword and waved it enthusiastically in the air.

"Set sail for the Deserted Island of Blossom!" shouted the Captain. "For we have strength and courage aplenty! But let's wait a few minutes, just to be sure *The Scavenger* is safely out of the way."

The Deserted Island of Blossom

ONWARDS AND UPWARDS. BUT MOSTLY UPWARDS.

The four sailors stood on a shore of golden sand. Behind them, *The Codcake* sat calmly at anchor. Beside them, their rowing boat lay beached beyond the reach of the tide.

"So this," said the Captain, "is the Deserted Island of Blossom."

In front of them, a sheer cliff of dull brown rock almost blocked out the sky. A few seagulls circled near its top.

"And that," said the Crew, "really is a tall cliff. Those seagulls up there are so small they look just like ants."

"Oh, yes," said the Penguin. "At least, like ants would look if they had wings and feathers and beaks like very, very tiny seagulls."

"And at the top of that really tall cliff," said the Captain, "is our prize. The fabled warbleflower."

The really tall cliff was so very really tall that they had to lean back to see the top of it – so far back that the Penguin slowly overbalanced like a skittle. He toppled over and flumped down flat in the sand.

"Just so you know," said the Penguin, "that was not funny."

"What we really need," said the Captain, "is someone who can fly up there to get the flower. Some sort of bird."

"Don't look at me," said the Penguin, flapping his flippers. "I don't do flying. Not since evolution. Underwater, I'm like a bullet. In the air, more like a brick."

"Time to climb," said the Captain. "Crew, Pinwing – you stay here. How's your head for heights, Cabin Boy?"

"Pretty good," said Eddy. But he was thinking that shinning up the climbing bars in the school gym was one thing, but this would be like taking on a skyscraper.

The Captain took off his long coat and folded it carefully, so that the carrot was snugly tucked away. Then he stepped forward to the base of the cliff. He put his right foot on a small bump in the rock face, and found a crack high to his left into which he jammed his hand. He heaved himself off the ground, and hunted with his left foot for something to take his weight. And then he fell off.

"Just practising," said the Captain.

"Perhaps this would help," said the Crew. She reached into her enormous red rucksack and pulled out a canvas bag. "Climbing ropes, spikes, a hammer – you know, the usual things. Just in case they came in handy."

"That was clever of you," said Eddy. "We had a demonstration once at school about how to use this sort of gear."

"First rate," said the Captain. "Then you can lead the way."

"Hang on," said Eddy. "I saw someone else do it, but I've never tried it myself. I don't know if I can."

"Nonsense," said the Captain. "Nimble lad like you

should have no trouble."

Eddy tried to remember what to do. He pulled out a long rope, a spike and a hammer, and slung the sack over his shoulder. He thwacked the spike into the crack in the rock, then tied one end of the rope to it, and clipped the other end to his belt.

"Here goes – I suppose," he said. He found a handhold on the rock and pulled himself up. Then he slowly leaned back to let the rope take his weight. He was relieved to find that he didn't immediately slither back to the ground.

"You see," said the Captain. "With this kit, getting to the top of this cliff will be easy as falling off a log. As long as we don't fall off, of course."

But it wasn't easy. Hammering spikes and tying off ropes made it slow work. Eddy felt like they had been climbing for hours.

"How high up do you think we are now?" he asked the Captain.

"Never mind that," said the Captain. "We just needs to keep on going right to the top. And remember, you must never look down, like this. Because if you do, you'll – oh my goodness…"

He clung to the rope and looked swiftly back up.

"…get very dizzy. We'll just have a moment's rest, while my head stops spinning."

He paused, and took several deep breaths.

"By the way, I reckons we've climbed about three times a man's height," said the Captain. "As long as he's a short one, that is. And not wearing a big hat."

"Is that all?" asked Eddy, rather disappointed. "We'll be climbing for a week at this rate." He silently wondered if they would ever make it at all.

"Onward!" shouted the Captain.

Eddy hammered another spike into the rock.

Slowly, slowly, they rose higher and higher.

And slowly, slowly, so did the sun.

The cliff face baked until it was almost too hot to touch.

Eddy's forehead was wet with sweat.

His throat was dry with thirst.

His shirt was sticking to his back.

His arms were aching. And all he could see above him was cliff and more cliff still to be climbed. *I can't do this,* he thought. *It's too much.*

But he couldn't just give up. He thought of the climbing bars in the school gym. Just a short scramble. A few rungs

at a time. Easy. That was the way
to tackle this cliff. Take it bit
by bit, not all at once.
Scramble by
scramble, totting up
his progress in his
head, Eddy made his
laborious ascent. Soon
he was almost level with
the circling seagulls.
Close up, the seagulls
didn't look at all like tiny
feathered ants. Or like
tiny anythings. Eddy had
never noticed before just
how big seagulls were –
especially when one landed
in a splutter of wings on a
ledge just above him. The
seagull let out a tuneless cry
and stared down at him with beady
orange-rimmed eyes. It didn't look
at all pleased to see him.

Please go away, Eddy thought. *This climb is difficult enough already.*

The seagull stretched forward and shouted loudly at Eddy. Then it pattered across the ledge to where Eddy's left hand had found a hold. It cocked its head to one side and eyed his fingers. Eddy suddenly realized that he had also never noticed before what sharp hooked beaks seagulls have.

"Oh, no," said Eddy. "You wouldn't."

But it would. The seagull thrust its head downwards, driving the point of its beak into the back of his hand.

"Ow!" shouted Eddy, and he instinctively pulled his hand away. This was not a good idea, for a reason which very quickly became obvious.

Gravity.

With a rush of terror, Eddy felt himself falling. He scrabbled at the rock face. His fingernails grated, but he couldn't find a grip. With a yell, he tumbled. As he fell, the last spike that he had hammered into the cliff flashed past his eyes. Had he done it right? Had he fixed it firmly enough to save him?

"Ooooooffff!" The breath was driven from him as the climbing rope strained against the spike – and held.

High above the ground,
he dangled in mid-air, his
heart thundering in his chest.

"Are you all right, boy?" he heard
the Captain calling.

"Yes."

His voice was a squeak.

The seagull dropped onto the top of
Eddy's head. It made a throaty chuckling
noise, and then started to jab its beak at the
climbing rope. Eddy saw with horror that it
was trying to cut through the threads.

77

Some of them were already fraying. If he didn't do something, it would soon be sawn through completely.

"Get off! Shoo!" he yelled at the bird, trying to scare it away. The seagull carried on pecking at the rope. Eddy reached up with both hands, and grabbed the bird. It jabbed its beak painfully at him again, but this time he kept his grip and hurled it away as hard as he could. The startled seagull thrashed through the air for a moment before it regained control of its flight, then wheeled away from the cliff with a screech.

Eddy hung an arm's length away from the rockface. He scanned it for a handhold and spotted a promising bump to the right – just out of reach. He kicked his legs hard, trying to set himself swinging, the effort making him feel hotter than ever. With a final wriggle he heaved himself far enough to grip the bump and haul himself across. He found a toehold to steady himself. Now he was taking his own weight again.

His arms throbbing with tiredness, the ends of his fingers rubbed raw by the rock, he dragged himself onwards.

When he looked up he could see the top of the cliff now, slashed across the clear blue sky.

Hand over hand he climbed, until suddenly there was no more rock in front of him, only sunlight and grass, and he flopped over and lay on his back, panting and laughing with relief.

A moment later the Captain crawled up beside him, gulping for breath.

"Well done, lad," he gasped.

"I thought I was going to fall," said Eddy. "When that seagull was attacking me."

"But you had courage and strength enough to climb to the top," said the Captain. "You passed Grungeybeard's test."

"You took your time, dearie," said a familiar voice close by. "I brought your coat, by the way. And two bottles of water. You look like you need them."

"What in the blue blazes?" gasped the Captain. "How on earth did you get here?"

"I took the lift."

"Lift?" spluttered the Captain, glugging down the cool water.

"The lift, yes. From the visitors' centre."

"Visitors' centre?"

"It's just between the two big hotels."

"Hotels?"

"Down where the tourist boats tie up."

"Tourist boats?"

"I'd like you to stop repeating what I say please, Captain dearie. It's getting very annoying. After you started climbing, I left the Penguin on the beach and went for a little walk. And just round the corner there's a marina full of tourist boats, and a visitors' centre with a lovely shop, and a lift so people can get up here easily. Let's face it, people are hardly going to be daft enough to try climbing that cliff, are they? Not when they're on holiday."

"Holiday?" gasped the Captain.

"You're doing it again."

"Tourists on holiday and hotels and shops and I don't know what! What's going on? According to the map, this is the Deserted Island of Blossom. De-ser-ted," the Captain repeated slowly.

"It must be a very old map. And the island must have changed over the years. Places do. I can remember when Tidemark Bay was surrounded by caravan parks. Now it's all just fields."

"And what have all these tourists come here touristing for?"

"The fabled warbleflower, of course. Look."

The Crew pointed behind the Captain. He and Eddy turned round, and saw a long queue of people waiting patiently to pass through a gateway in a tall barbed-wire fence. Uniformed stewards paced sternly on either side of them. They stood in the shadow of a huge sign, painted in bright red letters with the words:

WARNING! DO NOT TOUCH THE FLOWERS!!

"This is going to be a lot harder than I thought," said the Captain. "How on earth are we going to pick a fabled warbleflower with all those guards around?"

THERE IS NOTHING LIKE A GOOD PLAN

"To get that warbleflower," said the Captain, "we needs a plan."

"Can I just—" said the Crew.

"Shush!" the Captain shushed. "I'm the Captain and I reckon what we want is a really big cannon. KA-BOOM! We blast a hole in that fence and then snatch a plant."

"Problem," said Eddy. "We haven't got a cannon."

"If I could—" said the Crew.

"Shush!" the Captain shushed again. "Let me think. Got it! Plan B. We go and find a really big cannon. KA-POW!"

"But a really big cannon isn't something you just

find lying around," said Eddy.

"I've got a—" said the Crew.

"For the last time, shush! Maybe you're right about Plan B. So – Plan C. Two slightly smaller cannons."

"But—" said the Crew.

"Shush," shushed the Captain, "for the even laster time."

"Suit yourself, dearie," said the Crew.

"We need plan D," said Eddy. "D for diversion. Something that distracts all the guards. Then one of us can sneak in and steal the warbleflower while they aren't looking. What can we do to get their attention?"

"Well," said the Captain, "if we had a really big cannon…"

"Let's have a think," said Eddy.

"Who would like a sandwich?" asked the Crew. "Cheese and chutney. It was the very last one in the shop."

"Lovely," said Eddy. "It has been a long time since breakfast."

⚓ ⚓ ⚓

Seagulls are proud birds. Get the better of one and you can be sure that it won't forget. Which is why the seagull

that Eddy had met on the cliff was
now circling high in the sky above.
And why it had brought a mob of its
friends along. This was payback time.

The seagull checked its target, tucked
its wings in, and arrowed straight
down towards Eddy. The other birds
tailed after it, a plummeting cloud
of angry beaks, bent on revenge.
Eddy Stone had no idea what was
heading his way.

Just a feather's breadth from Eddy's
head, the seagull caught sight of the
sandwich. It flipped out a wing,
swerved past Eddy's right ear,
and fell on the food. The other
birds followed greedily,
screeching and squabbling, and
filling the air with angry cries, flying
feathers, and chunks of bread and
cheese. Eddy yelled at the gulls while
the Crew tried to drive them off
with a rolled umbrella.

The massive commotion turned every head in the queue of tourists. Guards left their posts and hurried over to try to sort it out.

"Brilliant!" the Captain shouted through the din. "I don't know how you organized it but that's what I calls a distraction, and no mistake. Warbleflower, here I come!" He set off at a trot.

It wasn't a very large cheese and chutney sandwich. The seagull had brought along a lot of friends. Approximately twenty-six-and-a-half seconds after the brilliant diversion had begun, the last scrap of food was gobbled up, the disturbance died down, the birds flew off, and the diversion suddenly didn't look so brilliant after all. Particularly for the Captain, who was way short of the gateway to the warbleflowers. He was still running at full pelt when he clattered into the two guards who'd stepped out in front of him. They lifted him by the back of his coat, and tossed him through the air over the heads of the people in the queue.

"And don't try that again!" the first guard shouted after him.

"We'll be looking out for you!" shouted the other, as the Captain hit the ground with a bump.

He limped back to where Eddy and the Crew were sitting in the middle of a drift of tattered seagull feathers and shredded sandwich wrapper.

"Right," he said, "who has an idea for plan E?"

"Well, if you've finished shushing, how about this, dearie?" The Crew pulled a plant pot from her bag. In it was a straggly little thing with spindly leaves and a few very small flowers of a drab pinky-brown-but-mostly-brown sort of colour.

"From the gift shop," she continued. "The fabled warbleflower."

"Is that what all the fuss is about?" asked the Captain. "It's not much to look at."

"Appearances aren't everything," said the Crew.

"Has it got a scent?" said Eddy.

"Oh, it has," said the Crew.

Eddy leaned forward and breathed in. It was like sticking his nose into an old trainer that had been worn by a wet Labrador that had trodden in something unfortunate.

"Just not a very nice one," said the Crew.

"Grungeybeard must have had a right laugh when he decided to make us go through all that trouble for such a boring little plant," said the Captain. He reached out to grab it, and…

"LA LA LAAAAAAAAAAAA!"

"Wow!" said Eddy. "It's singing."

"That's what they do," said the Crew. "I heard a few in the shop. All those people over there are waiting to hear the wild ones – apparently there are thousands of them on this hill."

At that moment, a high, sweet note trilled through the air. It was joined by another, and another, and then hundreds of them together, weaving melodies that rose into the bright sky.

"Lovely!" sighed the Crew.

"Fantastic!" said Eddy.

"Vocal vegetation is all well and good," said the Captain, "but we've got a quest to follow. Let's get this warbleflower back to the ship and find out from the map what our next challenge is. And this time we're all taking the lift down to the beach. Crew, lead the way!"

They passed a cow that was standing alone in a large

patch of daisies. The cow watched them as the lift doors closed. Then it said quietly, "Well, they did that the hard way, didn't they?"

"How would I know?" answered the cow's stomach. "All I can see is your rear end. It's my turn for the head next time."

Who was inside the cow suit? Were they members of *The Scavenger*'s crew, checking up on the Captain's progress? Were they spies who would soon be reporting back to whoever was behind the magic map? Or were they just two friends who like dressing up as a cow and who have nothing to do with the rest of the story?

CONTAINS <u>NO</u> CELERY

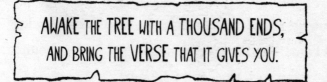

LEVEL TWO - THE ISLAND OF WORDS.

Back on *The Codcake*, the map wasted no time. As soon as the Captain placed the warbleflower next to it, it spelled out their next task. Eddy read out the words.

AWAKE THE TREE WITH A THOUSAND ENDS, AND BRING THE VERSE THAT IT GIVES YOU.

"What's that all about?" said the Captain. "How can a tree have a thousand ends?"

"Maybe it means branches and twigs," said Eddy.

"They are sort of ends."

"And we have to wake it," the Captain went on. "How do you wake a tree?"

"Bark," said the Penguin. "Come on, laugh. That was good."

"And how can a tree give you a verse?"

"It must be the Poet Tree," said the Penguin. "Get it? Poetry. I'm on fire. Someone should be writing this down."

"For once, I like that one," said the Captain. "The Poet Tree is what we'll call it."

"First a flower and now a poem?" said Eddy. "Is this Grungeybeard's sense of humour again?"

"He was a great one for poems, was old Grungeybeard," said the Captain. "He had verses specially written about how brave and brilliant he was. And about his true love – treasure."

"In love with treasure. That's not very romantic," said the Crew. "Not like having a sweetheart waiting at home, longing to see your ship sail into harbour. Have you got a true love, Captain?"

"The sea is my true and only love," said the Captain. "For what need have I of a maiden's lips when there is salt spray to kiss my cheeks? What need of soft words in my ear when the waves will lull me to sleep, or of warm arms when a tropical night can heat my bones."

"Never mind, dearie," said the Crew. "I'm sure you'll find a girlfriend eventually."

"Never mind saying never mind," said the Captain. "Just think about what lies ahead. You can bet your breeches that there will be another test to prove we are worthy of finding Grungeybeard's loot."

"How exciting," said the Crew. "I can't wait."

"You're going to have to wait," said Eddy. "It looks like it's a long journey to the Island of Words. We won't reach it before tomorrow morning."

"I can keep you all entertained with some jokes from my new act," said the Penguin. "What do you give to a fish with no ears? A herring aid!"

With a breeze in her sails, *The Codcake* followed a course to the Island of Words. The strange thing was that she did it without anyone steering.

"I think it's the map," said Eddy. "It must be telling *The Codcake* which way to go."

"Well I think," said the Captain, "that this old ship knows exactly where she's headed, and the map is just showing us."

"And I think," said the Penguin, "that if I end the act with a funny dance, the audience will love me. Hey – why don't prawns share things? Because they're a little shellfish!"

Waves slapped against *The Codcake*'s bow. The rigging clacked and the timbers creaked. And, loudest of all, the Captain's guts rumbled.

"My stomach wants a word," he said. "And the word it wants is not a polite one. What has happened to dinner?"

"I couldn't find any food in the hold," said Eddy. "But there was a big crate of leather boots. I've read that sailors sometimes boil those up when they are starving."

"That's no good to us," said the Captain. "In the first

place, we're nowhere near starving. In the second place, boiled boots taste disgusting. In the third place, they take about a day to cook, being as how they are tough as old boots."

"What about the ship's carrot?" asked Eddy.

"That carrot is a member of the crew," answered the Captain. "Eating other crew members is very bad manners."

"So is there no dinner?" asked Eddy. His tummy had started to feel very empty indeed.

"The life of adventure is not a life of comfort, lad," said the Captain. "But worry not, for we will have a Pirate Picnic. There may be no food on the table, but there is everything you can eat in your imagination. Think yourself full of dinner, and your hunger will vanish."

"Sounds unlikely," said the Penguin.

"Well, I'm willing to give it a go," said the Crew. "It's all part of the thrill of being at sea. And I'm sure my brain is more intelligent than my stomach."

Eddy concentrated. He thought burgers and baked beans and chips and ketchup. And then he thought cheese-and-peanut-butter sandwiches and jammy

Swiss roll and double-choc mint-chip ice cream.
With sprinkles.

"This isn't working," Eddy said. "It's making me feel more hungry."

"You can't just think of delicious stuff," said the Captain. "That only makes your stomach want another helping. The secret is to think of food you don't care for. Then your stomach decides it wants less. What about vegetables? I bet there's something you always leave on your plate."

"Only sprouts," said Eddy. "And cabbage, of course. Oh, and broccoli. And beetroot. And cauliflower and leeks and marrow and swede. And parsnips. And I'm not keen on spinach. Or radishes. Or broad beans or turnips or green beans or lettuce. And onions. Have I said sweetcorn? And runner beans and courgettes. And I just don't see the point of cucumber. But I eat all the others. It's like I tell my mum, I'm not a fussy eater, it's just that there are a few things I don't like. Oh, and celery. I really, really, really can't stand celery."

"Right then," said the Captain, "celery it is. Here goes." And he began to recite:

"We all had a pirate picnic
To feed our pirate crew
And on that pirate picnic
The food we had to chew
Was – CELERY!

"You next! Close your eyes and picture it. A big bowl of celery. Can you see it – all green and sticky?"

"Yes," said Eddy.

"Now sniff it – can you smell how it smells all celery-y?"

"Yes," said Eddy, screwing his face up.

"Imagine taking a big bite…"

"Ugh!" said Eddy.

"Now, remember all that and do the rhyme."

"Okay," said Eddy.

"We all had a pirate picnic
To feed our pirate crew
And on that pirate picnic
The food we had to chew
Was – CELERY! Yeuch!"

"Excellent," said the Captain. "Crew!"

"I've decided to make my imaginary celery into an imaginary soup," the Crew said cheerfully. "I've imaginarily fried it with bit of unreal onion, then pretended to blend it with made-up milk, tomato puree and a twist of black pepper – serve piping hot with make-believe warm bread and lashings of non-existent butter. Delicious."

"You've not really got the hang of this, have you?" said the Captain. "But you're a better imaginary cook than me. I even burn imaginary toast."

"That's enough imaginary celery for me," said Eddy. "I don't feel so hungry any more. I'm off to my hammock. Good night."

But Eddy couldn't sleep. His head was buzzing with the excitement of everything that had happened that day, and brimming with thoughts about what tomorrow might bring. He tossed and turned under his blanket for an hour, then decided to take a turn round the deck, to see if the sea air would help him to settle.

The western horizon glowed orange where the sun had almost dropped out of the sky to end the long summer evening. Lit by the last of its rays, the Captain stood gazing across the vast open sea. Eddy wandered across the deck towards him.

"Still awake?" said the Captain. "Perfectly natural on your first voyage. Feeling homesick?"

"No," said Eddy. "Here's much better. Anyway, I wasn't at home, was I? My mum and dad were too busy to be bothered with me. So why should I bother with them? Even when I am at home, they are hardly ever around. And when they are, it's always 'do this, do that'…'Get your homework done while I cook'… 'We're out of milk, pop down to the shops for me'… 'Your turn to clear up, I've got a pile of work to get through.' Always telling me what to do. I don't like people always telling me what to do."

"But now I tells you what to do."

"That's different. You're the Captain. It's your job to give the orders. And you're teaching me how to be a pirate and hunt for treasure."

They watched the sea together in silence. The western horizon was dark now. Thousands of stars perforated the clear night sky. The moon slashed its reflection across a calm sea.

"There's a lot of out there out there," said the

Captain. "It can be a lonely place."

"I'm not lonely," said Eddy. "Not now."

"No," said the Captain, putting a hand on Eddy's shoulder, "neither am I. You did well today, Cabin Boy."

"Thank you, Captain," said Eddy. And yawned. "I think I'm ready for sleep now. Good night."

He padded back to his hammock.

⚓ ⚓ ⚓

The eastern horizon was soon alight with a golden glow. But it wasn't because the sun had decided to make an early start on tomorrow. It was because Barracuda Bill had got bored, and wanted to have some fun. And the most fun he could think of was to set fire to a small island. A pretty island that had never done anybody any harm. A faint BOOM BOOM rolled across the sea as a thousand palm trees burned.

SOMETHING FISHY
IN THE AIR

Eddy slept with the scent of imaginary celery in his nostrils.

The next morning, he woke to the smell of fish.

Was this breakfast? He was starving. He jumped out of his hammock and looked around for signs of the catch. But there were none. Not so much as a sprat.

The Crew was asleep under a blanket on the deck. The Penguin was flat on his back, snoring gently. There was a loud BUMP as the Captain fell out of his hammock. His cabin door opened and he stepped out onto the deck, nostrils twitching.

"Fish?" he said.

The Crew opened her eyes.

"Fish? I'll find my frying pan."

"I can smell fish," said Eddy, "but I can't see any."

The Captain rubbed a finger across the deck. It came up shining in the morning sun.

"Fish scales," he said. "Fish have been here, where now fish are not. And as they do not usually jump out of the sea for a midnight stroll, someone must have brought them here. And if that someone wasn't one of you two…PINWING!!!!"

The Penguin sat up sharply.

"What do you know about this fishy fish business?" said the Captain.

"I have no idea what you are talking about," said the Penguin.

"Someone has been smuggling fish on board," said the Captain, "and I want to know who, how, what, why, when and where."

"Tut tut," said the Penguin. "Dear dear." And he burped.

The fishy smell wafted even more strongly across the deck.

"Aha!" said the Captain. "Let me smell your breath."

"I don't recommend it," spluttered the Penguin. "Brushing and flossing isn't my strong point – not with these flippers. You're not going to find a hint of mint."

The Captain bent over the Penguin and breathed deeply.

"Stinky fish!" he shouted, staggering backwards. "You stink of fish. You're as fishy as an octopus's armpit. What have you been eating?"

"A Pirate Picnic, same as you. Imaginary ocean snacks."

"We can all smell them."

"Well, I've got a very vivid imagination."

"The only thing round here that's fishier than your breath is your explanation."

"Oh, all right," said the Penguin. "What do you expect? I'm a penguin. When I'm hungry, I catch fish. Then I eat fish. Last night I was hungry. It's in my nature – you know what they say, fish gotta swim, birds gotta fly. Except that in my case, they were completely wrong about the flying part. I've gotta go fishing. It's just what I do. And anyway, what's the big problem?"

"You didn't share with the rest of us," said the Captain.

There was an uncomfortable silence.

"Well," said the Penguin. "You didn't give me any of your celery."

"Hrrump!" hrrumped the Captain.

"Grrump!" grrumped the Penguin.

"Pardon me if I'm speaking out of turn, Captain dearie," said the Crew, "but as Not Very Able Seaman Penguin has turned out to be Extremely Able Fisherman Penguin, and as we all want breakfast, why don't you make him our official supplier of fish?"

"Now that is an excellent idea," said the Captain. "Well, Pinwing, do you reckon you're up to the job?"

"Piece of cake," said the Penguin, slipping over the side of the ship. "Fishcake, that is," he added, as he plunged into the water.

"I'll just fetch that frying pan," said the Crew. "It's in my rucksack somewhere."

Before long, the Codcakers were sitting down to a delicious breakfast. Eddy soon felt full. And he didn't have to think of celery even once.

As soon as he had finished, Eddy checked the map. The drawing of *The Codcake* was getting very close to the Island of Words – a comma of land with a fat round body curling into a trim tail. He looked out to sea and…

The Island
of Words

"Hey, everybody! I can see the island!" Eddy shouted.

"No, no, no," said the Captain. "The words are 'Land ahoy!' Say it properly."

"Sorry," said Eddy. "Land ahoy!"

The Captain raised his telescope to his eye.

"That must be the Poet Tree," he said, "because it's the only tree on the island. It's right on the end point of the pointy end, and the pointy end is surrounded by even pointier rocks sticking out of the sea. There's no way to get the boat ashore there, but there's a lovely beach on the fat side, with some clumps of tall grass. So we'll land there and walk to the tree. Should be easy."

They would soon find out how wrong he was.

NOISE
ANNOYS

"Ow!" Eddy winced as a bamboo cane snapped back over the Crew's shoulder and landed a stinging blow on his cheek.

The clumps of tall grass that the Captain had seen through his telescope had turned out to be a lot clumpier than expected. The Codcakers were struggling painfully through a great wall of stems and stalks.

"It's quiet, isn't it?" said Eddy.

And it was. Strangely quiet. No birds twittered above their heads. No insects buzzed through the leaves.

"I hope you're not going to say 'too quiet'," said the Penguin. "Because you can bet that the minute you do some huge hairy beast will come roaring out of the bushes."

"It's called the Island of Words," said the Crew. "That doesn't sound like a place where huge hairy beasts lurk. You know the saying – sticks and stones may break my bones, but words will never hurt me."

"Huh!" said the Penguin. "That's rubbish for a start. Take my cousin. Words nearly killed him."

"I reckons I'm going to regret asking this, Pinwing," said the Captain. "But how on earth did words nearly kill your cousin?"

"Someone dropped a dictionary on his head. Knocked him out cold."

"I was right," sighed the Captain. "Everybody halt. I needs a rest to get my breath."

They stopped. The noise of four mouths gulping down the hot air filled Eddy's ears.

But wait. Could he hear another sound, too? He struggled to make it out.

"Hush," he said. "Everybody stop breathing."

"Slight problem," said the Penguin. "I get a medical condition if I stop breathing. It's called being dead."

"I mean, stop breathing for a minute," said Eddy.

"I think I can hear something."

They held their breath, and listened. It was faint, it was indistinct, but somewhere up ahead there was a definite rustling.

"The lad's right," said the Captain. "I don't know what's making that sound, but it could be part of the challenge that Grungeybeard has set. So let's be careful."

Slowly and cautiously, they pushed on. Just a little further ahead, the bamboo suddenly cleared. The Codcakers found themselves looking out over a wide, open space, as big as a football pitch. On its far side lay the end point of the pointy end of the island, a narrow, flat shoreline of brown pebbles. Above it towered a whopping great tree.

"The Poet Tree," said the Captain. "Let's get over there and see what's what."

The wide space in front of them was open, but it wasn't empty. It was covered in books – thousands and thousands of them, lying on their backs, their pages fanned out in the sun.

PONIES IN THE LOWER 4th

The Captain led the way, tiptoeing carefully through the books to avoid stepping on them. The noise that Eddy had heard was louder now. It was the sound of the breeze wafting their pages up and down, a gentle swoosh multiplied a million times over.

"It sounds almost like they are breathing," whispered Eddy.

"As if they were asleep," added the Crew.

"By the way," asked the Penguin, "WHY ARE WE WHISPERING?"

The Penguin's loud voice had a sudden and dramatic effect. The books that lay near his feet started to shake and shiver, their pages flapping wildly.

"They're taking off!" said Eddy. "Look – there – and there!"

Wherever he looked, books were quivering and wriggling and launching themselves into the air like a flock of clumsy birds. They swirled and flailed around the Codcakers, whacking into heads and shoulders.

One book hovered in front of Eddy's eyes, open at its first chapter. And then there was a voice. A rather old-fashioned voice. A rather loud voice, speaking the words that Eddy could see printed on the page.

"One bright sunny morning, Gerald the Pixie threw open the shutters on his front window, and looked out over Daffodil Dell..."

And another voice in his right ear...

"Please, Daddy! Sybil has a pony of her own. And Ethel, too. And simply everybody in the Lower Fourth except me..."

And another right behind him...

"'Mary, give everyone a big glass of squash,' Victor exclaimed commandingly. 'It's a hot day and the Superior Six are going to need cool heads, because I bet there's a great big mystery just around the corner.'"

In a moment, the handful of voices became a hundred, the hundred became a thousand, and the thousand became a great wave of noise that almost lifted Eddy off his feet. His head was spinning. He couldn't think straight. He took a deep breath and shouted "QUIET!!!!" with all the force in his lungs. But he couldn't even hear his own voice in the terrible din.

Then the pain began – as if a metal spike had been driven through each of his ears. And someone was drumming on the ends of the spikes with sledgehammers, banging them together inside his skull. His head felt like it was going to explode.

He had to make it stop. But the pain had driven all the ideas out of his brain. He didn't know what to do. He peered through the storm of flying books to try to see his shipmates. Perhaps one of them had come up with a solution.

The Captain was on his hands and knees, scrabbling in the sandy soil, digging a hole to bury his own head. The Penguin was standing completely rigid, his eyes staring blankly into space. The Crew had emptied a great pile of things that might just come in handy out of her rucksack, and had managed to stuff most of herself inside it instead. They weren't coming to the rescue.

Eddy's bones were shaking. The pain in his head was the worst he had ever felt, and it was getting stronger by the minute. He felt sick and dizzy. He was going to pass out. And if that happened, he doubted that he would ever wake up again. He had to do something.

But what?

STORY TIME

Eddy scrabbled at the laces on his baseball boots and yanked them off. Then he tugged his socks from his feet, balled them up and held them as tightly as he could over his ears.

That shut out some of the terrible noise. It was still horrible, but it was better – in the same way that having an agonizing toothache is better than having two agonizing teethaches.

Ducking low to try to avoid the storm of flying books, he headed to the heap of things that the Crew had taken out of her big red rucksack. What would

110

make thousands and thousands of books shut up? And then he had an idea. It might be a really useless idea – his head was in such a state that he just couldn't tell any more.

He hunted through and found what he wanted – a big, fat marker pen and large piece of stiff white cardboard. He had to let go of the socks he was pressing to his ears, which made it even harder to think what he was doing. But he managed to scribble the word *Silence* on the board. And he spotted a megaphone lying nearby – that would be helpful.

He stood up. Books battered and clattered into him, but he raised the board above his head with one hand, put the megaphone to his lips with the other, and bellowed: "This is not a zoo, it is a LIBRARY!!" Just like when Horrible Horrocks the scary school librarian shouted at his class during Quiet Reading.

The nearest books stopped talking immediately. Eddy heard the whisper "Library!" travel from book to book. He turned slowly round, holding the board. Silence flowed thickly across the field like a puddle of careless soup.

The great roar dwindled to a growl, then to a distant

purr. And then all was hush.

The Captain pulled his head out of the hole he had dug in the sand, and sat up, spluttering. The Crew clambered out of the rucksack, and started to tidy away all her things. The Penguin tugged a sardine from each ear and swallowed them thoughtfully.

"Blimey," he said. "I've heard of books being called volumes, but that was ridiculous."

The books had quietened down, but they were still flapping about.

"Which of you was the very first book to speak?" asked Eddy. A small blue book fluttered over to him.

"Not a word from the rest of you," said Eddy. "What was all that noise about?"

"I just want to tell my story," said the book, sounding sad.

A ripple of murmurs ran round the clearing.

"Me too."

"We all do."

"And what is your story?" asked Eddy.

"Ahem," said the book. "*Gerald the Pixie Paints His Shed*. Chapter One. One bright sunny morning, Gerald the Pixie threw open the shutters…"

"No," said Eddy. "Not every word. What happens?"

"Gerald paints his shed blue – his favourite colour. Then some naughty gnomes play a trick on him in the middle of the night and paint it red. When Gerald wakes up and sees it he decides that red is a very nice colour too."

"I see," said Eddy. "And then?"

"What do you mean 'and then'?" said the book. "The end. Page thirty-two. Look out for lots more lovely stories about Gerald."

"That's the whole story?" said Eddy. "I don't want to be rude, but it's a bit boring, isn't it?"

"Boring?" huffed the book. "Children loved Gerald. He has shoes with bells on the end that go jingle jangle and he sings his jolly jingly jangly shoe song. He was a big favourite. There are another 126 Gerald the Pixie books. Nice stories for nice children. *Gerald The Pixie Meets A Rabbit. Gerald The Pixie Has An Afternoon Nap. Gerald The Pixie Tries Toast.* How is that boring?"

"Well…" began Eddy, trying to work out how he could answer without hurting the book's feelings.

"And no one has read me since 1953," the book sniffled. "It's the same for all of us. No one has opened us for years. No one wants us any more." And it began to sob.

"I'm sorry," said Eddy. "That's not fair. It's not your fault that you are old-fashioned and dull."

"I'm afraid you can't force people to read what they don't want to," said the Crew.

"They do at school," said Eddy.

"That's different," said the Crew.

"Why?" said Eddy. "Is my geography textbook any less dull than, say –" he picked up a nearby book and read its title – "*Tilly's New Tutu*? …Okay, bad example."

"And what is wrong with *Tilly's New Tutu*," sniffled *Gerald The Pixie Paints His Shed*.

"It sounds wet," said Eddy. "What's it about?"

"How should I know?" asked *Gerald The Pixie Paints His Shed*.

"Hang on," said Eddy. "Do any of you books know each other's stories?"

"I shouldn't think so," said *Gerald The Pixie Paints His Shed*.

"And you all want someone to tell your stories to. So why don't you split up into little groups and take turns telling them to each other? And when you've finished, you can all swap round and do it again. Nice and quietly."

"I don't know," said *Gerald The Pixie Paints His Shed*. "Why don't we do that?"

Not one of the other books knew, either. So that's what they did. By the time Eddy had laced up his baseball boots again, all the books had arranged themselves in little circles, and the first of them had begun to tell their stories, nicely and quietly. A sound like ten thousand bees gently buzzing hung over the clearing, as the Codcakers headed towards the Poet Tree.

The whopping great tree was an even bigger whopper than it had looked from a distance. But as Eddy picked his way through the books that sat round its trunk, he could see that it wasn't looking well. Limp grey leaves hung from its drooping branches.

"The map told us to wake a tree with a thousand ends," the Captain said to Eddy. "And you reckoned that meant the ends of twigs. Well, this one has got at least a thousand of those. Besides which it's the only tree on the island. So what do you think we should do next?"

"I've no idea," said Eddy. "How on earth do you wake a tree?"

A LOT
OF GUTS

"Come on, you great leafy lump," the Penguin shouted up at the tree. "Stir yourself!"

"That doesn't seem to be doing any good," said the Crew. "And I think we've had quite enough loud noise for today, don't you?"

"Maybe there are some instructions for waking it somewhere," said Eddy. "Let's have a look round the trunk."

He stepped to his left, by a circle of books.

"…and they all lived happily ever after," came the voice of a tiny volume. "The End."

The End.

Awake the tree with a thousand ends.

"Captain," said Eddy. "I think I misunderstood what the map told us. I think it means that a thousand ends will wake the tree. The ends of stories. And all these books together should get through a thousand tales in no time. All we have to do is wait."

"Brilliant!" said the Captain. "As long as you turn out to be right, of course. If you turn out to be wrong, then it's completely daft. But I haven't got a better idea, so let's just wait and see. And while we're waiting... Crew! Pinwing! Keep an eye on this tree. Eddy, I am going to teach you something special. Something that you'll need to learn if you wants to be a proper pirate."

"Sound great," said Eddy. "What is it?"

"It's a game," said the Captain. "A game known and loved by every man who ever sought his fortune on the Seven Seas. A game of skill and nerve, of deep thinking and quick wits. And that game is called How Many Monkeys Have I Got In My Pocket?"

"Right!" said Eddy. "What are the rules?"

"The best way to learn is by having a go," said the Captain. "Now, you have to say to me – 'How many monkeys have I got in my pocket?'"

"Okay," said Eddy. "How many monkeys have I got in my pocket?"

The Captain stared into his eyes. Eddy stared back. The Captain raised his eyebrow, pursed his lips, furrowed his forehead and flared his nostrils. He thought for a moment, then said, "I think you have got two monkeys in your pocket. And now you tell me if I'm right."

"No," said Eddy. "You're wrong, I'm afraid. I haven't got any monkeys in my pocket."

"Mmmm," said the Captain. "I was close, though. Only two out. So. How many monkeys have I got in my pocket?"

Eddy looked at the Captain. Where could he have got a monkey from? And if he did have a monkey, wouldn't it be wriggling and chattering? At the very least, a pocket with a monkey in it would be bulging and lumpy, and the Captain's coat pockets hung flat and limp.

"I think you have got no monkeys in your pocket," he said.

"You're right," said the Captain. "Let's call that one a warm-up. Now for round one. How many monkeys have I got in my—"

"The tree!" the Crew interrupted. "Eddy was right!"

Book after book had reached the end of its story, and the tree had changed. Leaves that had hung limp and grey were now lush with green life. Branches that had drooped now pointed proudly to the sky.

"Looks like it's woken up," said the Captain.

"What are you going to do now, then?" said the Penguin.

"Who said that?" said the Captain.

"Me, obviously," said the Penguin. "If you look closely, you can see my beak moving."

"No," said the Captain. "The other voice. Listen, there it is again. I distinctly heard it say 'Come closer'."

"I can't hear anything," said Eddy.

"Nor me," said the Crew.

"Clear as eight bells," said the Captain. "And if I'm the only one who can hear the voice, I reckons that must be because I'm the only one the voice is talking to."

"What did you tell us about hearing the trees talking back?" said the Penguin. "Are you going gibbering, blibbering, babbling bonkers?"

"Quiet, Pinwing," said the Captain. "It's saying that to get a verse, I needs to tell the tree my most secret longings and desires, and it will turn them into poetry. I don't know what it's talking about. Secret longings, indeed."

"Everybody has secret longings," said the Crew. "It's the thoughts that come into your head when you're watching a beautiful sunset. Or standing for hour after hour staring at your auntie's terrible paintings and wishing that just one customer would come into your shop to buy something today. It's the things you whisper when you are pacing the deck alone at night – the ones you share with the waves and the wind, because you wouldn't tell them to a living soul."

"How do you know that I…?" the Captain began. "Right, you lot, keep your distance. If that's what I'm going to do, I don't want any of you trying to listen in."

The Captain pressed his face against the Poet Tree's trunk and spoke quietly – too quietly for anyone else to hear. When he had finished, he took a couple of steps back from the tree.

"What now?" said Eddy. "Is the tree saying anything?"

"Not a word," said the Captain. "I suppose we just have to wait."

They waited.

Nothing happened.

They waited some more.

Nothing did it again.

"If this is going to take a while," said the Captain, "I reckon we've got some unfinished monkey matters to sort out."

But at that moment, a dove flew down from high in the tree and perched on a branch just above him. It was carrying a large leaf in its beak. It cocked its head to one side, offering the leaf to the Captain.

The Captain reached forward and took it.

"It's got tiny words on it!" he exclaimed. "Well, not so much on it, like they were written in ink – more inside it, like they grew there."

"That must be your verse," said the Crew. "It really is a Poet Tree. Please will you read it to us, Captain, dearie?"

"They are my secret longings," said the Captain, "and they are going to stay my secret. We've got the poem that we were sent here for. What's in it is my private business." He carefully tucked the leaf up his sleeve.

Its delivery completed, the dove launched itself from its perch and flew straight upwards. As it rose, it let out an enormous wet poo that splashed on the Captain's hat and then splattered onto the ground.

"If there's one thing I can't stand it's a mucky hat," said the Captain. He went quietly to the shoreline, took his hat off and dipped it in the sea.

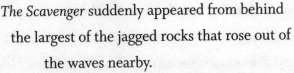

BOOM BOOM

The Scavenger suddenly appeared from behind the largest of the jagged rocks that rose out of the waves nearby.

"I do love sneaking up on people," Barracuda Bill shouted from *The Scavenger*'s deck. "It always makes me laugh

122

when they jump like that. I saw your little ship anchored over there, and I thought you might be able to help me with a question. And that question is – have you seen a cow anywhere round here? WELL?"

"A cow?" the Captain shouted back. "Not that I remember."

"If you do, make sure you tell me. Something is going on that I don't know about and I do not like that one little bit. Come to that, what are you up to on this island?"

"Just washing my hat," the Captain answered.

Bill snorted with laughter. Two dozen huge and hairy pirates who were on deck with him joined in.

"Cleaning up, eh? Well, it's a good day for little jobs."

"He doesn't seem so bad, really," the Crew whispered to Eddy.

CRACK! Bill whipped a flintlock pistol from his belt and fired it into the air.

"I'll tell you when you can speak! Next time, I'll take aim," he snarled. "Funnily enough, we're cleaning up, too. We've bailed out the bilges and swabbed down the decks, and now we're going to put the rubbish out. Ready, lads?"

"Aye, Skipper," the hairy pirates replied.

"Right – an extra tot of rum for anyone who hits the one with the mucky hat!"

The pirates pulled catapults from their pockets and blunderbusses from their boots. A furious volley of fish heads and fish guts and one mouldy yellow sprout flew towards the Captain.

SPLAT! The fish heads spattered onto his green coat. SPLURT! The fish guts squelched into his red-and-white striped breeches. PING! The sprout bounced off his shoulder and parted Eddy's hair as it flew by.

"I reckon that's extra rum all round!" shouted Barracuda Bill. His horrible cackling laughter rang out over the loud BOOM BOOM of the pirates' feet stamping on *The Scavenger*'s deck as they sailed away from the island.

"Oh, dear," said the Crew. "I'm afraid we're going to have to wash more than your hat, Captain."

"That man is a menace," said the Captain. "Him and his whole crew."

"You have to admit though," said the Penguin, "their aim is impressive.

I never thought they'd hit you from that distance."

The Captain shook off his long boots, then peeled off his green coat and pulled off his striped breeches.

"If there's two other things I can't stand," he said, dunking the clothes in the water, "it's a mucky coat and mucky trousers. And while these are drying, we'll have that round of How Many Monkeys."

"That might be difficult," said Eddy. The Captain was standing on the shore wearing only his long undershirt and moth-eaten socks. "Right now you haven't even got any pockets to put your monkey in." At least that meant they wouldn't have to play the silly game again, thought Eddy.

"Good point," said the Captain. "But I'll beat you next time."

"Why is Barracuda Bill so horrible to you?" asked Eddy.

"He's horrible to everyone. And the reason why he's horrible to everyone is that he's just plain horrible. He's as bad as a quarrel of crocodiles and as mad as a bee in a bottle. I heard tell that on one island he visited, he stole all their food to feed his crew."

"That's bad," said Eddy.

"And then he made everyone wear their underpants over their heads, banned Wednesdays, and ordered them to say everything backwards."

"And that's mad," said the Crew.

"Let's just hope that's the last we see of him," said the Penguin.

"He has a nasty habit of turning up where he's not wanted," said the Captain. "Which is anywhere. And if he finds out we're looking for Grungeybeard's treasure, then we'll really be in trouble."

IF FIREWORKS HAD FLAVOURS

"Yum!" said the Captain. "Chocolates. I like a good choccy. Just like Grungeybeard. He were famous for his sweet tooth."

"The map said we've got to collect them," said Eddy, "not eat them."

"Yuck," said the Penguin. "Gooey sticky muck. Give me a nice bit of fish any day."

A few hours had passed since the Captain had shown the verse from the Poet Tree to the magic map, and the map had revealed the next stage in the quest:

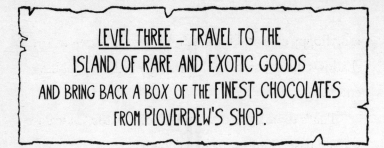

The poem was now safely stowed in the shabby old sailor's chest in the Captain's cabin, *The Codcake* was safely docked in the harbour on the Island of Rare and Exotic Goods, and the four adventurers were standing on a quayside that hummed with noise and bustle. Wherever they looked, people were loading crates and baskets and boxes on and off ships.

"Right," said the Captain, "let's find this sweet shop."

"And look out for anyone selling socks," said Eddy. "I must have left mine somewhere in the middle of all those books."

The Codcakers pushed past market stalls laden with strange-looking fruit and vegetables. Eddy spotted one that was piled high with punnets of tiny orange berries, and bunches of what looked like bright blue bananas. A woman had baskets of hot cakes that steamed with sweetly spiced aromas. Another had a pen full of – well, Eddy would have called them ducks if they hadn't had

128

long floppy ears and big feathery paws. Hidden in the shadows nearby stood a surprisingly ordinary-looking cow.

"That's them," the cow said quietly as the Codcakers walked past. "Keep your head down."

"My head is already down," grumbled the stomach. "I thought it was my turn to be the front this time?"

"We could do with some directions," said the Crew. She walked up to a merchant who was wearing a long yellow coat and a jewelled eyepatch. "Excuse me, can you help us? We are looking for chocolates."

"Chocolates? No," he replied. "But I have some beautiful necklaces made of hens' teeth." He threw the coat open, to reveal a dozen strands of polished white spikes dangling from his neck.

"I'm sure they are lovely," said the Crew. "But we are trying to find Ploverdew's sweet shop."

The man shrugged his shoulders and pointed. "Down that street."

"Thank you," said the Crew. Eddy looked down the narrow street of brightly painted buildings.

"I can see the sign," he said.

"Ploverdew's. At the far end on the left. Come on!"

"You three go," said the Penguin. "I'll catch you up. This is so much better than sweets."

The Penguin was gazing at a huge tank of water in a shop window. Tiny coloured flashes darted and dabbled between waving weeds. They were fish – but fish like he had never seen before, as bright as the blocks in a paintbox.

"Hellooooooooo!" said the Penguin. "Oh, my!"

Eddy was the first to reach Ploverdew's shop. He peered in through the dusty window at a banner that promised: *Try our treats and you will never go anywhere else again.* The room beyond was lined from floor to ceiling with dark wooden shelves, and the shelves were lined from side to side with clear glass jars, dozen upon dozen of them. And every jar glowed with colour – orange and ochre and scarlet and green and black-and-white stripes and pink-and-purple swirls shone in the dull interior of the shop.

"First in the shop gets to choose," said Eddy. "Anyway, I bet I know much more than you two about sweets."

A bell jangled as they opened the door and stepped

inside. Footsteps pattered up a set of stairs, and a head appeared over the counter.

"May I help you, good sirs and madam?" asked the shopkeeper. He had a small thin voice, which suited his small thin body and small thin head. Above his small thin mouth was a small thin nose on which perched an enormous pair of spectacles.

"We want some sweets, please," said Eddy.

"To describe the creations in this shop as 'some sweets' is like describing an exquisite painting as 'some brushmarks', or a beautiful symphony as 'some notes'," the shopkeeper sniffed. "We do not sell 'some sweets'. I, Lanceling Ploverdew, pride myself that these are the finest sweets. Our every product is a delicious morsel of confected perfection, a masterpiece of mouth-watering lovelitude."

"There's so much to choose from," said Eddy. "I can't decide where to begin."

"I was always partial to wine gums," said the Crew.

"Perhaps madam might be tempted by our vintage selection," said Ploverdew. "We use only the finest wines from the finest years, aged in our cellars until they are at their peak, and then – well, why waste words, when you may try one sweet each before you buy?" He unscrewed the lid of a jar, reached in with a white cotton-gloved hand, and offered a sugary crimson jewel to the Crew.

"Thank you," she said, and popped it into her mouth, "Mmm – it's really very very…" She made satisfied sucking noises.

"I believe you will find lavish blackberry fruit with notes of cedar and cinnamon, and a hint of sunburnt leather. I believe you may reflect that compared to this delectable delight, other wine gums taste like a mouthful of sheep dip – with the sheep still in it."

"Mmmmmmm," the Crew nodded as she sucked, "sssss vrrrrrr goooooo."

"Precisely." Lanceling Ploverdew smiled and turned to the Captain. "I deduce from the cut of sir's garmentage and the lingering tang of dead fish in the air that sir is a nautical adventurer – does sir know he has a carrot on his shoulder, by the way?"

And from another jar he drew a dark brown pearl.

"So – from distant lands. Cocoa beans grown by a jungle tribe. Antique rum salvaged from a storm-wracked galleon. A hint of nutmeg from the forests of an uninhabited volcanic island – the east slope, just below the waterfall, where the spice is caressed to extra ripeness by the early morning sun. All in glorious harmony in our lushest, smoothest, velveteen truffle."

"A choccy," said the Captain, as he popped it in his mouth and chewed. A look of dreamy surprise came over his face, his jaw slowed, and he began to roll his tongue round the scrumptious mouthful.

"And for young sir, perhaps a sherbet fountain?" Ploverdew took a tube of brightly coloured paper from a cabinet, placed it in Eddy's hand, and tore a small cardboard lid from its top. The tube puffed a cloud of orange powder into the air. Eddy was so surprised that he completely missed it, but he stuck his tongue out in time to catch a gush of green that zinged his taste buds with a fizz of grape. Then came yellow pineapple, and scarlet raspberry, each more intense than the fruitiest fruit he had ever tasted.

"Wow!" he giggled. He lay on his back on the shop floor, holding the sherbet fountain above him as blasts of tangerine and plum and blueberry tumbled one after the other into his open mouth.

If fireworks had flavours, Eddy thought, *I mean, if flavours looked like fireworks…* And then with a final puff of peach the tube collapsed, and all he could think of was that he had never really tasted anything before in his life.

"That was very," said the Crew. "Very very very very."

"Mmmmm," agreed the Captain, smacking his lips together. "As sure as fish have fins. I want another one."

"Me too," said the Crew.

"And me," said Eddy.

"Of course you do," said Lanceling Ploverdew. "That was 'try before you buy'. Now it's time to 'buy after you've tried'. You have money, I presume?"

"Oh," said Eddy. "I spent all mine on a shabby old sailor's chest."

"Oh," said the Crew, "my three doubloons went in the gift shop on the Deserted Island of Blossom."

"This here is our funds for the voyage," said the Captain, pulling a leather purse from his pocket, and emptying the contents onto the counter. "Three golden guineas, five doubloons, six ducats, a handful of silver and – what's that?"

"It looks like a Choccy Puff," said Eddy. "I wonder how that got in there."

"I'm robbing myself," said Ploverdew. "But as I like you, I suppose that will do."

"All of it?!" exclaimed the Captain.

"Oh, yes," said Ploverdew. "Though not the Choccy Puff. Nasty tacky icky sticky horrid vulgar thing." He brought his fist down on it.

"For three sweets?" asked the Captain.

"Chocolate from the jungle, fine vintage wines and antique rum do not come cheaply. Not to mention the genius behind the exploding fruit sherbet fountain – my genius – inspired, unique, and precious. But if you don't want…"

"But we do. We do," the Captain, the Crew and Eddy interrupted anxiously.

"Of course you do," said Ploverdew, sweeping the money into a drawer and the remains of the Choccy Puff into a bin. He took a silver tray and laid out one wine gum, one truffle and one sherbet fountain. The three fell greedily on the sweets, chewing and sucking and smacking their lips in pleasure.

This time, Eddy was ready and hunched over his

treat to avoid missing a single speck of powder. Once again, he was completely taken over by the zinging tingling fruitiness, until the tube gave its last puff of peach and folded in on itself.

Then the fruitiness faded on his tongue, the tingle dwindled, and the zing went zonk.

Eddy suddenly felt horribly empty. The world seemed grey and drab. There was only one thing that would make him feel alive – really alive – again.

He had to have another one.

He had to have another one.

He

Had

To

Have

Another

One.

ANOTHER ONE

"I have to have another one," said Eddy.

"I have to have another one," said the Captain.

"I have to have another one," said the Crew.

"I know," said Lanceling Ploverdew. "Do you have another purse?"

"You've had all our money," said the Captain.

"What a shame," said Ploverdew. He pulled a heavy metal shutter down in front of the shelves where the jar of wine gums stood.

"No!" shouted the Crew. And she burst into tears.

"But yes," said Ploverdew. He locked the cabinet where the sherbet fountains were lined up.

"Another one!" shouted Eddy, trying to scramble over the counter.

"Although," said Ploverdew, "you could always do some work for me, and I could pay you with sweets. If, of course, there's nowhere you have to go." He smiled a joyless smile.

"Go?" said the Captain. "Who would be daft enough to want to go anywhere when there's sweets like these to be had?"

"We'd love to work," agreed Eddy.

"Wine gum," said the Crew.

Lanceling Ploverdew opened a door behind the counter and beckoned them through. They trooped down a set of rickety wooden stairs into a cold and dingy cellar, where twisted glass tubes bubbled with thick coloured liquids and oddly shaped jars held rainbow clouds of swirling vapours.

"Now," he said. "Who wants another sweetie?"

Eddy knew that he had never in his life wanted anything so much.

"Me!" he shouted. "Me! ME! *ME!!*" as the Captain and the Crew joined in.

"And what will you do to earn one?" asked Ploverdew.

"Anything!"

"That's what I like to hear. Start with that enormous block of chocolate in the vat over there. Turn on the heat and keep stirring once it begins to melt."

The three Codcakers pushed and shoved each other to get at a giant wooden spoon.

"I'm so glad you dropped by," said Ploverdew. "My last lot of helpers were quite, quite worn out, poor things. So keen to get their rewards that they worked themselves to death."

And then he laughed a brittle, brutal laugh. A laugh so icy that it would have chilled a curry. A laugh that almost stopped him hearing the jangle of the shop doorbell.

Almost. But not quite.

"Curses," cursed Lanceling Ploverdew. "I hate being interrupted in mid-evil. Still – more customers. And where there is work for three there is work for more."

He turned towards the stairs. "Let me go and see who will be the next to join our merry band."

⚓ ⚓ ⚓

The Penguin was not in the best of moods. First, he had found out that he wasn't allowed to eat the little fishes.

Their owner had explained this to him using a large and painful fly swatter. Now, he had come into this sweet shop to find no trace of his shipmates.

"They couldn't even wait for me," he muttered. "If there's one thing I can't stand, it's impatience. And just how long does it take to get some service in this place?"

"Sir?" Lanceling Ploverdew slipped through the door behind his counter. "May I be of assistance?"

"About time," huffed the Penguin. "I'm looking for the three people who came in here a few minutes ago. Hairy one with a carrot on his shoulder, an old lady and a boy."

"Oh, yes, sir. They left."

"Without me," said the Penguin. "Isn't that charming?"

"Oh, dear. How tiresome. Might I offer sir a little something to cheer him up?"

"Don't mind if you do," said the Penguin.

"I see that sir is a native of the frozen lands – so, a reminder of cooler times?" Ploverdew laid a snow-white cluster in front of the Penguin. "A tingling mingling of arctic cloudberries and white chocolate made with reindeer milk. And if you have ever

140

tried to milk a reindeer you will know why this is so very special."

"Got anything with a bit of fish?" asked the Penguin.

"Fish?"

"You know. Shiny slippery swimmy things."

"I know what fish are. Slimy scaly smelly – eurggh!"

"Says Mister Reindeer Milk. What could be more delicious than some lovely haddock éclairs? Mackerel marshmallows? Shrimp gums?"

"Revolting!"

"Just the thought of them makes me drool."

"Stop dribbling on my floor, you feathered freak."

"Who are you calling a feathered freak?"

"Let me look around. Ah! You are the only one with feathers here, so Mister Freaky must be you."

That did it. The Penguin wasn't going to put up with being insulted any longer.

"Now listen here, sugarbreath…" he began.

"Well?"

"I mean…" Come on, he must be able to think of something. A witty insult to cut the old humbug down to size. "Errrr…" But nothing would come. Still, people often said that actions speak louder than words. So he

blew a loud raspberry, lowered his head,
launched himself forward, and sank his
beak into Ploverdew's skinny leg.

"OWWWWW!"

The Penguin's charge propelled them
both through the door behind the counter.
The sweet maker shot away from the
impact, cannoned into the handrail at the
top of the stairs, toppled wildly
backwards, and teetered for a
moment in mid-air.
He scrabbled to
grab hold of
something –
anything. But his
fingers only clawed at
empty space. With a terrible screech he fell
down and down and down until with a loud
FLOOOOOMMMP! he landed in the huge
vat of now-melted chocolate.

"Well, that's shut him up," said the Penguin with a satisfied grin.

But it hadn't. Ploverdew raised his chocolate-coated head from the thick brown pool.

"A sweetie for whoever eliminates this pestilent penguin!" he shouted.

Three shadows emerged from the gloomy reaches of the cellar. As they approached the stairs, the Penguin recognized them. The Captain, Eddy and the Crew. What on earth were they doing, messing around down here?

"Oi! You three! Let's grab some chocolates and get out of this dump!"

They started climbing towards him. They were talking, but too quietly for him to make out what they were saying.

"Speak up," said the Penguin. "I can't hear you."

And then, as they got closer, he did hear them. Quite distinctly.

"Get the Pinwing," said the Captain.

"Get the Pinwing? I mean, Penguin?" said the Penguin. "Why would you want to get me, guys?"

"Sherbet," said Eddy.

"Choccy," said the Captain.

"You'd get me, just for a sweet?" asked the Penguin.

"No contest," said the Crew.

They were almost on him now. The Penguin knew that he could try to get away, but they could run a lot faster than he could waddle. In fact, they could take a gentle stroll, with frequent breaks to have a nice cup of tea and admire the scenery, a lot faster than he could waddle.

"Guys," he said, his voice shaking a little. "It's me. Your shipmate. Think of all the happy times we've had together, like…okay, think of all the times we've had together. You wouldn't do anything to hurt me, would you?"

"Get the pinwing, get a sweetie," said the Captain.

The Penguin backed towards the door.

"Snap out of it!" he said.

"Sweetie," said Eddy.

"Can't you think of anything but sweets?"

"Yum!" said the Crew. "Get the Penguin."

The Penguin stepped back again – and felt the closed door behind him. He was trapped against it, with nowhere to go.

Still they came towards him, their eyes mean, their stomachs greedy, their hands outstretched to...

"Get

the

Penguin."

A GREEN AND STICKY SITUATION

"Oh, brilliant," said the Penguin. "Is this how it's going to end? All because you lot can't think with your brains instead of your stomachs."

Brains?

Stomachs?

What did that remind him of? Something he'd heard before.

He dodged as hands grabbed at him, but it was no good. They were pulling at his feathers, tugging on his flippers, clutching at his – ouch! And then he remembered. It was what the Crew said that night on the ship when there was nothing to eat – that her brain was more intelligent than her stomach. Maybe the trick that worked then would work now, too, and break the spell of the sweets. He took a deep breath and shouted as loud as he could:

"We all had a pirate picnic
To feed our pirate crew
And on that pirate picnic
The food we had to chew
Was – CELERY!"

There was a flicker in Eddy's eyes, he thought. A tiny movement of the lips.

"Celery!" the Penguin shouted again. "Great big green sticky bunches of the stuff!"

Eddy's nostrils twitched. He could almost smell it.

"C-l-y," he mumbled.

He could almost taste it.

"C-l-r-y."

He didn't like it.

"Celery."

Funny, thought Eddy. He was sure he had been thinking about something else. Something not celery.

Oh well, he would probably be able to remember it if it was important. Just like he would probably be able to remember where on earth he was. And what on earth was going on.

"Hello, Penguin," he said. "What are you doing?"

"Trying to stop you three scuppering my promising showbiz career," said the Penguin.

"I see," said Eddy, though he still didn't. "Where are we?"

"Pinwing, what is happening?" asked the Captain.

"Got any celery?" asked the Crew.

"It's good to have you back," said the Penguin.

"Have we been away?" asked Eddy.

"Yes, you have been away," said the Penguin. "What on earth did you think you were doing?"

But before anyone could answer his question – or rather, before anyone could say that they hadn't a clue what the Penguin was going on about, because they couldn't remember anything that had happened since they came into the shop – they were interrupted by a voice from below. An angry voice. The voice of someone who had been dipped in chocolate from a great height.

"Misshapes! Rejects!"

They looked down from the stairs. A sticky, drippy, brown figure was slowly hauling itself upright.

"Who is that?" asked Eddy.

"That is Ploverdew," said the Penguin. "And before you ask, yes we are in the back room of his sweet shop, no he is not happy, yes I pushed him in, no it wasn't an accident, and yes I do think we should be going."

"Not so fast!" shouted Ploverdew. His clothes had soaked up gallons of chocolate, which made them tremendously heavy. But struggling and grunting with effort, he managed to clamber out of the vat and onto the cellar floor. Warm chocolate rolled slowly down his body and began to form a glistening puddle around him.

"You will never get the better of me! You see this handle – all I need to do is pull it and KA-BLAMMO!"

"Ka-BLAMMO!?" said the Captain. "What's ka-BLAMMO!?"

"You are about to find out," snarled Ploverdew. "Say goodbye!"

He reached for a bright red handle that jutted out from the wall in front of him. Eddy watched as

Ploverdew started to tug on it – and then everything seemed to turn into slow motion – and then slower motion – and then motion so slow that even a particularly lazy snail would have suggested putting a spurt on. Until, finally, the motion stopped altogether.

The warm melted chocolate had soaked into Lanceling Ploverdew's clothes. It had covered every inch of his skin. It had left his hair standing up in little chocolate thickets. Now, in the cold air of the cellar, it was cooling down. And as it cooled, it hardened. The world's finest and most evil sweet maker was completely stuck in a thick chocolate shell, an utterly delicious one-man tailor-made prison.

"I aaay oooo aaaaaa!" he growled between rigid lips.

"Should we help him?" asked Eddy.

"Definitely not," said the Penguin.

"But he could be stuck in there for ever."

"I don't think so. Look."

As they watched, Ploverdew forced the tip of his pink tongue out between his teeth, and began to lick round his chocolate-coated mouth.

"But by the time he eats his way out, we'll be long gone," said the Penguin. "Move it."

"Hang on a moment," said the Captain. "Is it just me, or does anyone else want to pull that lever and find out what ka-BLAMMO! is?"

"It's just you," said the Penguin, pushing through the door and back into the shop. "Let's grab the goodies and go."

The Crew picked up a large purple box of chocolates from the counter.

"They look lovely," she said. "Who would like a taste?"

"Promise me," said the Penguin, "that you three will never, ever, try one of these sweets."

"Why?" asked the Crew. "What could be the harm in that?"

"You really don't remember what happened in here, do you?" asked the Penguin.

"Not a thing," said Eddy.

"I'll fill you in on the way back to the ship," said the Penguin. The bell on the door jangled as they stepped out into the street. "It's an exciting story about an incredibly brave and heroic Penguin."

But they were going to have to wait to hear it – because what they found outside froze the words in his beak.

BACKWARDS
SPOKEN ARE
SENTENCES
SOME

The market of rare and exotic goods had been devastated. It looked like a herd of angry buffalo had stampeded through. A herd of angry buffalo driving steamrollers.

The stalls had been overturned, their wares scattered and trampled across the cobbled quayside. Tiny orange berries and bright blue bananas were pulped into puddles. Floppy-eared ducks scuttled about on feathered paws, pecking at crumbs of sweetly spiced cakes. And all around the stallholders sat on the ground, cowering and silent. With their underpants over their heads.

"What happened?" said the Crew.

"You mean, *who* happened," said the Captain. "Listen!"

From out at sea came the faint but unmistakable **BOOM BOOM** of *The Scavenger* sailing off to spoil someone else's day.

Eddy recognized a long yellow coat – though last time he had seen it the man wearing it hadn't been hiding his face under a pair of purple pants.

"Are you all right?" he asked.

"Buffalo angry of herd stampeding a like was it," the man answered, almost sobbing. "Everyone at shouting brute horrible a by led."

"And then he ordered you to put your underpants on your head and say everything backwards."

"Week the of day favourite my was Wednesday," the man added sadly.

"It's okay," said Eddy. "They've gone now."

"Sure you are?" asked the man.

"Really sure," said Eddy.

The man pulled the pants from his head. He blinked in the sunlight, and then began to pick up the bright white hens' teeth that lay scattered around him.

"He asked if we'd seen a cow," said the man.

"The cow again?" said the Captain. "And had you?"

"Yes. Earlier. But by the time he asked us it had gone. And when he couldn't find it he got angry."

"I don't know what this cow business is about," said the Captain. "But I do know that when Barracuda Bill gets angry he's even more dangerous than usual. Let's just hope we can steer well clear of him from now on."

⚓ ⚓ ⚓

"…and you all woke up with no idea what you were doing." Back on board *The Codcake*, the Penguin finished explaining what had happened in the evil sweet shop.

"So if it hadn't been for you," said Eddy, "we'd still be stuck in there."

"You were the hero of the hour," said the Crew.

"I like the sound of that," said the Penguin. "I think I've found my perfect role. The brave and handsome hero. The great guy who the ordinary people thank for saving them."

"Thank you, Pinwing," said the Captain.

"Don't mention it," said the Penguin. "I don't mean that, obviously. Do mention it, as often as you like.

Or even as often as I like. You know, this is the first time I've ever felt properly appreciated. I think this must be what it's like to be happy."

"You mean you've never been happy?" said the Crew.

"There was a Thursday at the Ocean Park," said the Penguin. "One of our keepers slipped on a stray herring and fell over. We all sat on him. That was about as good as it got. And speaking of herring, I'm off to catch dinner." He slipped over the side of the ship.

The Crew pulled the box of chocolates out of her rucksack.

"That's the third item for our quest successfully collected," she said.

"And the map said that we had to collect four things to show we were worthy of winning our prize," said Eddy. "So that's only one more to go."

"Let's take these chocolates over to the map so we can find out what the last challenge is," said the Captain. "And then we'd best put them away safely."

The Crew pulled two padlocks out of her big red rucksack.

"We can lock them away in your chest, Captain, dearie. If you and I each have one of the keys, we won't be able to break in and try them if we're tempted again."

"How do you manage to be so organized?" asked Eddy.

"It's experience," said the Crew. "A lifetime of it."

"I wish my gran was like you. She's had loads of experience too, but it just seems to have worn her down."

"None of us can choose how we get old, dear. I'm just lucky that I can still get on with my life. Although I didn't have much of a life to get on with before I came on this adventure."

The chocolates had an immediate effect on the map. Eddy read the new words that scrolled out across it.

"It's real treasure this time," he exclaimed. "It says,

LEVEL FOUR – THE ISLAND OF FEAR.
BRING BACK A RUBY RING FROM
THE EMPEROR'S CASTLE."

"Rubies were Grungeybeard's favourites," said the Captain. "He had a ruby ring for every finger. And on the biggest of them he had a skull engraved with a letter 'G' in one of its eyeholes. But I reckons this will be difficult. I don't like the name of that island. And I don't care for the look of that castle."

The drawing on the map showed a stout-walled stronghold protected by a moat and drawbridge.

"In fact," added the Captain, "I don't see how it could be more difficult."

"Look," said Eddy, "there are more words appearing."

"Ah," said the Captain. "So that's how it could be more difficult. Let's make sure to get a good night's sleep and keep our wits about us when we get there tomorrow.

We were slapdash today. We should have found out about Ploverdew before we went charging in."

"But it all worked out in the end," said the Crew, "thanks to the Penguin."

"I heard that," said the Penguin, who had clambered back on board with a pile of sleek silver fish. "Say it again. Applaud if you feel like it."

"The map shows a creek running up to the middle of the island near some woods," said the Captain. "We'll break out the rowing boat and come at the castle from there. There's three ways with walls – over, under or through. I'll decide which way is best when I've had a good look and a good think."

"Don't forget you've got me with you," said the Penguin. "The hero. I reckon I'm ready for anything that island can throw at us."

But he wasn't.
No one was.

FRIENDS
AND FOES

"Remember, everybody," the Captain ordered, "keep your eyes peeled and shout out at the first smell of a monster."

"All I can smell is fish." Eddy sniffed the air as he rowed the little boat up the creek.

"We can all smell fish, dearie," said the Crew. "Which is not surprising because we all smell of fish. That's what eating it three times a day does for you. And of course you, Captain, are particularly pungent after Barracuda Bill pelted you with all those fish guts."

"Enough chatter," said the Captain. "Watch out for danger signs."

The creek cut through a sunny meadow dotted with flowers. They passed a dandelion patch, where rabbits flopped and lolloped. They swished under a weeping willow, where blue and orange birds swooped. They stepped ashore by a patch of tall grass, where purple butterflies flitted and fluttered. They tied their boat to a bleached wooden post, on which was nailed a board painted with bright red letters that said: DANGER!

"We've found one," said Eddy.

"Best take a good look round before we make a move," said the Captain.

The Crew pulled a pair of binoculars from her rucksack and handed them to him.

"Twin telescopes. Very neat," said the Captain. He scanned their surroundings.

"I can't see any monsters," he said. "Hang on. Back along the creek. Can you see what I'm seeing?"

He passed the binoculars to Eddy.

"That's really odd," said Eddy. "I wouldn't have thought you could even get a cow into a canoe, let alone teach it how to paddle. Do you think that's the cow that Barracuda Bill is after?"

"Could be," said the Captain. "And if it is, I want to know what it's up to." He started waving in the cow's direction. "Hey! You! Mooo!"

"That's done it," said the front end of the cow.
"They've spotted us. I told you that this disguise only
blends in when we're on land."

"It's the only one we've got," said the back end. "You
want to dress up as a giant squid, you get the sewing
machine out."

"Oh, stop arguing and keep paddling."

The cow began to turn the canoe clumsily and head
for the far bank of the creek.

"Let's get after it," the Penguin urged heroically.

"Should we follow it?" asked Eddy. "Or head straight
for the castle and the ruby ring?"

Before the Captain could answer, a sudden cry
stopped him dead.

"Halt! *Qui va là?* Who goes there?" a shrill voice
demanded.

"Who said that?" asked the Captain. There was no sign of the owner of the voice.

"I asked first," it replied.

"Perhaps the monsters are invisible," said the Penguin, suddenly sounding rather less heroic.

"Friend or foe?" asked the voice.

"I can't answer that if I don't know who you are," the Captain replied.

"So, you refuse to identify yourselves. *En garde!*"

"How can I '*en garde*' when I can't see you?"

"Here we are," said the mystery voice somewhere near his right ear. "Before I make you wish you had never been born, allow me to introduce myself. I am the Chevalier François Cabernet Lalande-de-Pomerol, and this is Plonque, *mon ami* and companion in blood."

"*Bonjour!*" said a second tiny voice.

"We are the
Raisins of Death!
Attack!"

Eddy saw two tiny
blobs leap from the top
of the danger sign, and
land on the Captain's hat.

"Ha ha!" the two voices cried together, as the raisins began to jump up and down.

"Do not bother to beg for mercy, dog!" the Chevalier yelled.

"Fair enough," said the Captain.

The raisins jumped up and down some more.

"He's a big one," said Plonque, panting slightly. "It would be easier if he took his hat off. Do you think we could ask him?"

"*Courage, mon brave*, and alley-oop!" replied the Chevalier. And he began to jump higher and harder.

"I think," said Plonque, "I need a bit of a rest."

They stopped jumping.

"The Raisins of Death?" asked Eddy.

"Indeed," said the Chevalier. "The most feared and fruity assassins in all the island."

"*Oui*. That's us," said Plonque.

"And how does that work, then?" asked the Captain.

"We jump on your head till it breaks and – poof! – you are dead," explained the Chevalier. "So! Now you are afraid – no?"

"Not really, no," said the Captain.

"He has spirit, this one," said Plonque. "Not to mention a very thick head."

"We haven't got time for all this," said the Captain. "We've got to get to the Emperor's castle."

"The castle?" said the Chevalier. "And what exactly is your business there?"

"What business is it of yours what our business is?" said the Captain.

"It is the business of *la Résistance* to know all the business concerning the Emperor – may his undergarments itch intolerably. We are sworn to overthrow his cruel tyranny – and in the meantime to think up as many ways as we can to get on his nerves."

"Then you shouldn't be fighting us," said Eddy. "We're here to break into the castle—"

"And slice him into tiny pieces?" asked the Chevalier.

"Not quite," said Eddy. "To steal a ruby ring."

"Tiny pieces is better," said the Chevalier. "But the ring will do."

"Then maybe you can help us?"

"Our enemy's enemies are our friends. And your companion with the thick head is very brave – he did not flinch when we set about him. He did not snivel to be spared. Just the sort that *la Résistance* needs. So of course we will help you."

"First, we need to get inside his castle," said Eddy.

"Aha! We know a special way," said the Chevalier. "Come with us."

"That map is rubbish," said the Penguin, as the raisins led them through a wood. "The first island that's supposed to be dangerous is the first island that isn't. Here be monsters, indeed."

"You've perked up again," said Eddy.

"If two bits of dried fruit are all it has got, then I reckon this is the perfect place to be a hero."

They reached the edge of the wood. The Emperor's castle stood before them, gloomy and glowering over the landscape.

"The defences are strong," said the Chevalier. "But sharp brains can pick the lock that would defeat brute force. Come."

He led them to the foot of the wall, took a deep breath, and then shouted, "What is the difference between the Emperor and a bucket of horse manure? The bucket!"

"What is he doing?" asked Eddy.

"Insulting the Emperor – may he get shampoo in his eyes at bathtime," said Plonque.

"Why is the Emperor's face like lumpy mashed potato?" shouted the Chevalier. "I don't know why, it just is!"

"I like it," said the Penguin. "But I'm not sure they can hear you inside. Let me have a go, this is right up my street. Stand back everybody – it's hero time. I'm not saying the Emperor is stupid," he yelled, "but if brains were dynamite, he couldn't blow his hat off!"

"That's very good," said the Chevalier.

"Here's another," said the Penguin. "What is the – hang on, where did the ground go?"

The ground had not gone anywhere. But the Penguin had. Hoisted into the air, his flippers flapped in the breeze. He couldn't see the hand that had lifted him, but the other Codcakers could – at least, they could see the studded leather glove that the hand was wearing. And they could see the shining chain mail covering the massive muscular body that the hand belonged to. And the featureless helmet that covered the face of the guard who was now dangling the Penguin in mid-air.

Even worse, they could see the guard's thirty brawny companions, because they were now surrounded by them.

With a snarl and a grunt, the first guard slung the Penguin over his shoulder and stomped off towards the castle gate. His thirty companions silently lowered thirty vicious-looking spears and prodded them at the other Codcakers.

"I think," the Penguin shouted back at them, "they want you to follow us."

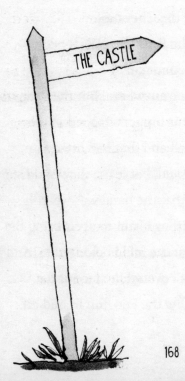

THE CASTLE

THINGS GO REALLY BADLY

The heavy gate slammed shut behind them. They were standing in a large courtyard, its high walls made of dull grey stones that seemed to suck the sunlight out of the air. Eddy shivered in their shadow. He looked round to see if there was any way to escape – supposing they got a chance to escape – but the Emperor's castle appeared to be as impossible to break out of as it was to break in to.

The guards raised their spears and stepped back. Their leader tossed the Penguin off his shoulder. He sailed through the air with a squawk and landed at Eddy's feet.

The Penguin picked himself up, dusted himself down, and said, "If that's flying, you can keep it. It's rubbish."

"*Voilà*," said the raisin Chevalier François Cabernet Lalande-de-Pomerol. "We are inside the Emperor's castle, just as I promised."

"You forgot to mention that we would be under armed guard," said the Captain. "This is bad."

"No – our position is excellent," said the Chevalier. "Now we have tricked them into bringing us here, the most difficult part is over. All that remains is to overpower these brutes – and what is that to a man of courage like you? And then we will decide what unpleasantness to inflict on the Emperor – may his bed sheets always have crumbs in them."

"Never mind crumbs," said the Captain. "We're in a right pickle. There's a difference between courage and stupidity, and trying to fight these guards would definitely be stupid."

"Sorry to break up your little chat," said a voice behind them.

They turned to see a smiling young man in a smart purple uniform.

"You must be the new prisoners," said the young man. "Lovely to meet you. As you will see from my badge, my name is Robin, and I'll be your Prisoner Orientation Officer – or P.O.O. for short."

"I'm glad you explained that," said the Penguin. "I wondered why you had Robin Poo on your jacket."

"A joke," chuckled Robin. "Well done, you. Not many prisoners manage to keep a sense of humour. Now, I'm here to guide you through the trial and punishment process. So, any questions – fire away!"

"Trial?" said the Captain.

"And punishment?" added Eddy.

"Punishment, yes," said Robin. "After you are found guilty."

"Not us," said the Crew. "We've done nothing wrong."

"And another one," laughed Robin. "You guys crack me up. Everybody who is put on trial here is found guilty. It's a very efficient system. And then you get executed."

"Executed?" said the Penguin.

"Executed, punished, whatever. Same thing. But now we really must get on. Follow me, please."

A menacing shake of the guards' spears persuaded the Codcakers to do as Robin asked. He led them into a vast hall, thronged with people. More guards stood in front of the iron bars of a prison cell.

"Now," said Robin, "if you could just pop yourselves in there for me? I'm sure the Emperor won't be long. Don't worry about the paperwork, I'll handle that – and any last words and personal belongings you would like sent to your loved ones." And with a cheerful wave, he left the guards to shove them into the cell and bolt the door.

"This is now badder than bad," said the Captain.

"It is superb!" piped up the Chevalier. "It is our chance to inspire *la Résistance*. They will speak of how we comrades stood together behind the brave pirate Captain who laughed in the face of the Emperor and challenged him to do his worst."

"Well," said the Captain. "Maybe not his very worst."

"They will paint pictures of us!" the Chevalier continued. "They will tell their children stories about us!"

"All about how we were horribly executed. Very nice for the kiddies," added the Penguin.

"Shhh!" said Eddy. "I think he's coming!"

CLACK CLACK CLACK.

They heard the sound of boots clumping down a corridor.

CLACK CLACK CLACK.

With a mighty blare of trumpets and a cry of "Make way for the Emperor!" the crowd in the room broke into cheers and applause and a flurry of curtsies and bows. Some of them bent so low that they touched the floor with their noses.

Peering through the throng, Eddy saw a very short man wearing a very large crown enter the room. He was dressed in a velvet jacket studded with precious stones, embroidered silk trousers, and soft leather slippers that padded silently across the floor. Behind him walked two uniformed servants. One carried a large slab of marble. The other held a leather boot in each hand, which he beat on the marble slab to make the sound of the heavy footsteps that had announced the Emperor's approach.

The Emperor padded towards a tall throne at the end of the room. Finely dressed ladies scattered rose petals at his feet. Caged songbirds twittered as he passed. Exotic perfumes were sprayed into the air. Trays of delicious nibbles and glasses of thirst-quenching cordials were offered to him. The Emperor would have needed a heart of stone not to be delighted by the elaborate show.

And a heart of stone was just what he had. He kicked the rose petals aside. He shouted at the birds to shut up. He coughed at the perfumes, spat out a nibble and dashed the drinks to the ground. When he reached the throne, he turned. His face was a scrunch of bad temper.

"Useless!" he yelled. "You're all useless! Who do I have to waste my precious time on today?"

Robin stepped forward. "There's a trial, Your Magnitude. Prisoners."

"Oh!" said the Emperor, sitting down and perking up. "That's more like it. Have they been very bad?"

"That's for you to decide, Majesty."

"Yes it is, isn't it?" He rubbed his hands together and turned to the prison cell. "Well, what have you villainous vermin got to say?"

"What are we supposed to have done?" asked Eddy, his voice trembling.

"You are supposed to have obeyed the law, of course.

If you don't know that you must have been very badly brought up. But this trial is not about what you are supposed to have done. This trial is about what you have actually done."

"And what have we actually done?"

"You tell me," said the Emperor. "You were there. You saw it all. You know all the wherefores and whys. So. Speak up." He sat back, looking very pleased with himself. The whole room broke into applause.

"A very subtle line of questioning, Your Immensity, if I may say so," said Robin.

"Yes, it was rather brilliant, wasn't it?" agreed the Emperor.

"All we did was land on the island," said the Captain.

"Aha!" said the Emperor. "So, you admit the whole dastardly plot. You invaded the Empire, no doubt intending to seize the throne, paint a moustache and funny glasses on my portrait, and rob my poor subjects of their beloved Emperor."

"Oh, stick it in a sandwich and choke on it," a raisiny voice piped up from the prison cell. "Your subjects hate you."

"As you have not tried to bore me with a lot of

pointless facts, I shall be merciful," the Emperor continued. "The sentence is death."

"You call that merciful?" said Eddy.

"However," added the Emperor, "because you are so very smelly, I have decided to double the sentence. That fishy whiff is horrible. And let that be a lesson to you next time."

As the room broke into applause again, the Chevalier squeaked, "Now is the moment, Captain. Now you can laugh in his face."

"I don't see the joke," said the Captain.

"It was the one about not being found guilty, remember?" said Robin cheerfully.

"What will happen to us?" asked Eddy. His voice wobbled in his throat.

"Well," said Robin, "the Emperor has to decide how to have you killed. With a bit of luck, it will be swift and painless."

"Executioner!" the Emperor shouted. "Bring in The Beast!"

"Ah!" said Robin. "Oh, well, never mind."

THINGS GET EVEN WORSE

It wasn't quite the roar of a lion, and it wasn't exactly the rasp of an electric saw, and you wouldn't have mistaken it for the slobbering of a huge dog, but there was a bit of all three in the terrible noise that was coming along the corridor.

Something heavy was being dragged along. Something that didn't like being dragged along and was going to make sure that everyone had got that loud and clear.

AAARGHHHNNNNAOOOOOW-AAAAARGLELOBBLYSLARP.

The Codcakers all knew that this must be The Beast. They didn't know what kind of beast it was, but they were all sure that they were going to find out far, far too soon, and that when they did they would wish they hadn't.

Four guards staggered into the hall, grunting and sweating as they hauled an iron cage on wheels behind them.

The creature inside the cage was nowhere near as small as a lion. Its teeth were far less blunt than an electric saw. Its drooling jaws were not as dry as a slobbering dog. And as for its appearance…it wasn't just the mean look in its bloodshot yellow eyes, the greasy green fur that hung in matted clumps like a filthy rug, the black tongue that lolled out of its slack slavering jaws, the torn and dirty claws sticking out of its huge front paws, or the crust of snot around its scaly snout. No, it was the way that all of these combined that made it so hideous.

That, and the farting.

The Beast, whatever it was, was a thing that only its own mother could love. And even she would have needed to be half-blind and to have lost her sense of smell.

PHHHHLAARRRRRP!

A waft of old cabbage and bad eggs spread through the room.

"And he said *we* smelled bad," said Eddy.

"Behold!" the Emperor shouted. "The mighty Beast! Has it been fed?"

A man in a zookeeper's uniform with a black hood over his head stepped out from behind the cage.

"Not since yesterday, Majesty."

"Excellent – hang on, are you the zookeeper or the executioner?"

"Both, Majesty. You fired the previous pair."

"Oh, yes. They were useless," said the Emperor. "So it must be hungry."

"It's very rude to talk about me like I'm not here," said the Beast, in a sulky voice. "I can speak for myself."

PHHHHLAARRRRRP!

"From both ends, unfortunately," said the Emperor. "Beast, are you hungry?"

"Might be," said the Beast. "Depends."

"On what?"

"Don't know."

"Is something wrong with it, Keepercutioner?

179

I mean, Exezootioner?" said the Emperor. "It seems very moody."

"It's at a difficult age," said the Exezootioner.

"You're doing it again," grumped the Beast.

PHHHHLAARRRRRP!

"Put the cage in position," the Emperor commanded.

The guards pushed the Beast's cage up to the Codcakers' cell, with their doors in line.

"*Vive la Résistance!*" squeaked the Chevalier. "You may kill our bodies, but you will never kill our spirit!"

"The bodies are quite enough for me, thank you," replied the Emperor. "Guards – release the Beast!"

The guards raised the door on the Beast's cage. All that stood between the Codcakers and the terrible jaws of the farting Beast was the door of their own cell. And the guards were already lifting the catch that held it in place.

Eddy could feel his heart thumping as if it was trying to break out of his chest.

"Goodbye, Captain," said the Crew. "It has been an

honour to serve with you. I'd like to say it has been a pleasure as well, but in the circumstances that would be idiotic."

"I'm sorry," said the Captain quietly. "Our story wasn't meant to end like this."

The prisoners huddled together as the cell door slid aside. The Beast lifted its broad bottom, let out an enormous blast of wind, and shambled towards them. They could smell its hot breath, as fragrant as a roasted dustbin. The Beast loomed over them, its jaws dripping.

Eddy pressed himself tight against the Captain.
He felt a hand grasp his and squeeze it hard. His body
was jangling with energy, yelling at him to run away.
But he was caught in the cell, with nowhere to go.

It was all wrong. He shouldn't be here. He should be
on holiday with his parents. His stupid parents who
were always too busy. He thought of his dad and that
way he always hogged the TV remote. And his mum,
who still pulled his socks up like he was a toddler. His
mum. She would never even know what had happened
to him.

"Mum," he said quietly.

Eddy closed his eyes and waited for the snap of jaws.
The chomp of teeth. He hoped it would all be over
quickly. Please let it be over quickly.

LOVELY CRUNCHY HEADS

Eddy flinched as he felt a string of sticky drool land in his hair and run down his face. The Beast pressed its snot-crusted snout against his cheek and took a deep sniff.

Eddy screwed his eyes tight and waited for the bite.

But nothing came.

He lifted one eyelid and peeped out.

"It's fish," said the Beast. "Don't like fish."

"What do you mean, it's fish?" asked the Emperor. "Look at it. It's three human beings and a weird bird."

"And two deadly raisins," yelled the Chevalier and Plonque.

"It stinks like fish. I'm not eating it."

"It's got legs," said the Emperor. "When did you ever see a fish with legs?"

"There are lots of things that I've never seen," the Beast answered in a sad voice. "Balloons. A windmill. The seaside."

The Beast flumped back on its fat smelly bottom, a picture of misery.

"Never seen the seaside," said Eddy. "Poor you."

"It's just dungeon, cage, dungeon, cage, day after day," said the Beast. "Never any fun."

"That's so sad," said Eddy.

"Stop that," said the Emperor. "I know what you're doing. You think that if you pretend to feel sorry for the Beast he won't want to eat you."

"I already don't want to eat him," huffed the Beast, "because he is a fish."

"How can he be a fish?" asked the Emperor. "He's got clothes on."

"Clothes. Batter. Breadcrumbs. What's the difference?" asked the Beast. "They disguise your food but one bite and – yuck. It's still fish."

"There's no fooling you," said Eddy. "Inside these

clothes we're all yucky fish. Isn't that right, guys?"

The Codcakers all loudly agreed, and tried to look as much like fish as possible. Which is quite hard, when you think about it.

"Don't listen to them," said the Emperor.

"I'm not listening to *you*," said the Beast.

"Come on, just bite the heads," said the Emperor. "Lovely crunchy munchy squidgy heads. You know they're your favourite bits."

"Shan't."

"You can have ketchup."

"I want pizza."

"Stop being stupid and eat your dinner!"

"No! I hate fish and I hate you!"

"For the last time – they are not fish!!!" the Emperor screamed at the top of his voice.

"I'm going to tell my mum," said the Beast.

That stopped the Emperor in his tracks.

"No don't do that," he said hastily. "We've only just finished rebuilding after the last time she got angry. You don't have to eat them. Guards, take him away. Keeper, give him a pizza if it will keep him quiet."

"I want spicy sausage on it," said the Beast, flopping

back into his own cage, "but no olives. They're almost as horrible as fish."

Eddy let the air out of his lungs in a great whoosh of relief. The palms of his hands were sticky with sweat, and his heart was still thumping as the guards dragged the Beast's cage away.

He was glad that his heart was still thumping. It meant that he was alive. Alive – but not free.

The Emperor looked as if he might explode with fury at any moment.

"I want these prisoners chained up in the dungeon while I think up a really horrible way for them to die, which I can't do right now because I'm too upset. Bring me the Head Jailer!"

"Tiny problem," said Robin. "You sacked him for feeding the prisoners too much bread with their mould."

"Then get the Deputy Jailer," said the Emperor.

"Sacked," said Robin.

"The Guard Sergeant."

"Sacked and chained up in cell number three."

"Who is running the dungeon, for goodness' sake?"

"Old Ichabod," said Robin, checking the details on

his clipboard. "He's the only one left down there."

"Old who?"

"Ichabod. He's in charge of prison catering. His job is to get today's bread before it goes to the prisoners and lick off some of the mould. Then he licks it onto the stale bread that's going to be tomorrow's rations, so it will grow nice and furry by the time we feed it to them."

"You'd have to be a halfwit to do that."

"Oh, he is," said Robin chirpily.

"Very well," said the Emperor, "bring him to me."

"Slight hitch," said Robin. "He hasn't been out of the dungeon for twenty-three years. He has grown terrified of daylight. Goodness knows what would happen if we dragged him up here."

"Why is everybody except me so useless?" said the Emperor. "I've a good mind to sack the entire population and get a new one."

"Well, you know what they say," said Robin. "If the fool in the dungeon won't come to the Emperor, the Emperor must go to the fool in the dungeon."

"If I hear them say that, they will find themselves chained to the wall next to the Guard Sergeant."

Eddy's brain clicked into action. Maybe this was an opportunity to trick their way out of trouble.

"There's no need to put yourself to any bother, Your Magnificence," he said. "We can make our own way to the dungeon." Once they were out of sight, they would be able to slip away and try to escape. But would the Emperor fall for it?

"I'm not going to fall for that, you cheeky little squirt," said the Emperor. "Even if it means I have to take you to the dungeon myself. The sooner you are securely chained up, the sooner I can decide how to get rid of you for good."

24

DOWN IN A DUMP

The way to the dungeons was dark and damp. Led by the Emperor, and watched by a pair of armoured guards, the Codcakers trudged along passageways carved into the rock, climbed down stairs slimed with fungus, and breathed air stale with misery.

As the steps descended, so did Eddy's spirits. He wondered what horrible fate the Emperor was going to dream up for them. The same worry gnawed at the other Codcakers. None of them spoke a word.

They turned a corner. Ahead of them a bulky iron door blocked their path. Next to it was a large sign surrounded by twinkling fairy lights, and painted with bright orange letters which read:

ABANDON
HOPE
ALL YOU
WHO
ENTER
HERE.

Eddy stared at the smiley face in the "o" of "you".

"That was my idea," said Robin. "The old sign was just boring old black. I think this really cheers the place up."

One of the guards stepped forward and hammered on the door with his mailed fist. It boomed like a drum that summoned the prisoners to their doom.

CLUNK – a heavy bolt was drawn back.

RATTLE – a chain was pulled aside.

"Hang on a minute," said a croaky voice on the other side of the door.

CLUNK. RATTLE. CLUNK. CLUNK. RATTLE.

Finally, they heard the scrape of a key being pushed into a lock, the squeal of rusty metal as it was turned, and another scrape as it was pulled out of the lock again.

"Wrong key," said the voice.

SCRAPE. SQUEAL. SCRAPE.

"I know it's here somewhere," said the voice.

"Try the one with the label that says *Dungeon*," Robin shouted.

"All right," said the voice. "But you'll have to wait a bit."

"For goodness' sake, how long?" yelled the Emperor.

"Depends," said the voice. "How long does it take to learn to read? Hang on, I've got a better idea. I'll try this shiny one."

Another scrape, another squeal. The lock clicked and the door swung open with a grating groan.

The dungeon beyond was even gloomier than the passage. As Eddy's eyes adjusted to the murk, he made out a large pile of hair in the doorway.

Two hands emerged, and parted the thick mane to reveal a grimy and wrinkled face. This must be Ichabod, Eddy realized, twenty-three years after his last haircut and shave. A toothless mouth said, "What is it?"

"Prisoners," said the Emperor.

"No thanks. We've already got some," said Ichabod, turning to go.

"Do you know who I am?" shouted the Emperor.

"Why? Can't you remember?" asked Ichabod. "Poor you. It's terrible when you lose your…um…remembery wotsit."

"Useless," said the Emperor.

"You can't talk to me like that," said Ichabod. "I'm in the service of the Emperor."

"And I am the Emperor."

"There you go. You've remembered who you are. That's nice." Ichabod smiled a gummy smile.

"Listen very carefully, you numbskull," the Emperor replied through gritted teeth. "Here are my orders. Number one – take the prisoners and chain them to the wall of the dungeon. Number two—"

"You missed out number three," Ichabod interrupted.

"I'm doing number two," snarled the Emperor.

"Well, it's very confusing."

"Why do I have to put up with this? I'm the Emperor. I should be up in my palace Empering. Instead I'm down here doing bad counting with a hairy halfwit."

The Emperor turned in a tantrum and kicked out at the nearest available object. His soft-slippered toe met the guard's heavily armoured leg with a loud crunch.

"Owwwwwww!" The Emperor hopped around on his good foot.

"Sorry, Your Splenditudinousness," the guard muttered anxiously.

"Did that hurt?" enquired Ichabod, as the Emperor continued to howl.

Eddy wondered if they could take advantage of the confusion and get away. But he was disappointed to see that the second guard was watching them intently, spear at the ready. He was even more disappointed when he spotted two small blobs skipping unnoticed past the guard and away up the steps. The raisins! So much for the Chevalier's talk of comrades standing together bravely, he thought. They were running away and abandoning the Codcakers.

The Emperor stopped hopping and howling. But he carried on being cross with Ichabod.

"The only thing saving you from unimaginable misery and pain is the fact that there is no one else witless enough to want your job. Now repeat after me. One – chain the prisoners to the wall."

"One – chain the prisoners to the wall."

"Two – keep them chained to the wall."

"Two – keep them chained to the wall."

"Three – wait for orders."

"Three – wait for orders – and lick the bread."

"And remember this – they may have dangerous accomplices who will try to release them. Trust nobody. Above all, give the keys to nobody. Those are my orders," said the Emperor. "Follow them to the letter."

"What letter? No one told me there was post," said Ichabod. "But there's no point giving me a letter on account of the not-reading thing."

"Oh, get me out of here," said the Emperor. "Just remember. Chain, chain, wait. Trust nobody. Give the keys to nobody. A child of seven could do it."

"Not me," said Ichabod. "I was a bit dim when I was little. Still, I got there in the end. Chain, chain, wait, nobody. See. I won't let you down."

"I'm going now," said the Emperor, "to order a nationwide hunt for another idiot who likes mould." He stomped off.

"Now that's all sorted," Robin said to the Codcakers, "I'll just give you this customer satisfaction survey. If you would like to fill it in for me when you've got a minute that would be lovely. Don't leave it too long, though, because – well, you haven't got too long, have you? Still, it's been fabulous working with you."

And he trotted after the Emperor.

The two guards glared at the prisoners.

"Now," said Ichabod, "chain. I think that's right. Yes. Chain. And let's get a move on. Bread doesn't lick itself."

As they were led away, the Captain whispered, "Don't worry, me hearties, with this nitwit in charge, we're sure to be able to escape. Mark my words – we'll be out of here in five minutes, or my name isn't Captain Jake McHake."

25

NOBODY
ESCAPES

The good news was that the Crew had been smart enough to pack a lock-pick, a hacksaw and a large file in her red rucksack full of things that might just come in handy.

The bad news was that the guards had been smart enough to put the red rucksack well out of reach before chaining the Codcakers up and marching back upstairs.

"Rumpelstiltskin? Walter Wobblebottom? Crown Prince Percy of Pomerania?" shouted the Penguin. "Five minutes to get out of here, you said, or your name is not Captain Jake McHake. You've been tugging at those chains for at least two hours and here we are still padlocked to the wall. So come on, who are you? Arthur Mometer? Terry Dactyl? Alison Wonderland?"

"Whatever happened to Mr Cheerful the pinwing hero?" asked the Captain.

"He got sentenced to death and strung up in a dungeon," the Penguin answered glumly. "I'm going to stick to expecting the worst from now on. It's less disappointing."

"Let's face it," said Eddy. "The only way we'll ever open these locks is with the keys."

KERCHING! Eddy suddenly had an idea.

"So, let's get the jailer to give them to us," he said. "Jailer!"

"He's cracked," said the Penguin.

"Hush," said Eddy. "Just keep quiet, all of you. Jailer!"

The hairy haystack that was Ichabod shuffled into view.

"Give me the keys so we can leave," said Eddy.

"Do you think I'm daft?" asked Ichabod.

"We haven't got time to discuss that," said Eddy, "just hand them over."

"No," said Ichabod.

"Oh, dear," said Eddy. "You are going to be in so much trouble. Remind me – who did the Emperor tell you to give the keys to?"

"You can't catch me out," said Ichabod. "He told me to give the keys to nobody."

"Correct," said Eddy. "Allow me to introduce myself. My name is Horatio Nobody. I am the Imperial Inspector of Prisons, and my colleagues and I are here on a surprise undercover visit. I'm pleased to say that we are more than satisfied with what we have seen. The dungeon is filthy, the chains are uncomfortable, and the whole experience is truly miserable – just what we want for our prisoners. So well done, inspection over, give me the keys and we'll be on our way."

"But nobody is supposed to get the keys." Ichabod sounded even more confused than normal.

"Exactly. And here I am. Horatio Nobody."

"Prove it," said Ichabod. "Show me your documents."

"I don't carry documents when I am working undercover. But the other staff of the Prison Inspection Department can confirm my story. And look – here they are, hanging on the wall next to me."

"Oh, yeah, so they are. That's a stroke of luck, isn't

it?" said Ichabod. "Now listen, you three. Is what he's just said right?"

"Oh, yes," answered the Crew. "I can definitely say that Nobody is telling the truth."

"Me too," said the Captain.

"No question," said the Penguin.

The Codcakers could almost hear Ichabod's brain cells grinding. Finally, he said, "Pleased to meet you, Mister Nobody," as he passed the keys to Eddy.

Most of the keys had no labels on them, but it took less than five minutes of trial and error to fumble through them and unlock the chains.

"You won't mention our little misunderstanding to the Emperor, will you?" asked Ichabod anxiously, as Eddy handed the keys back to him.

"I can promise you that we won't breathe a word," said Eddy. "Our work is top secret. Speaking of which, we don't want anyone to see us leaving. I don't suppose there's a back entrance to this place, is there?"

"Only the tunnel under the moat that leads to the hidden gate in the forest," said Ichabod. "Would that do?"

"That," said Eddy, "sounds perfect."

Ichabod led them down a side passage. After a few strides, they passed a heavy door. It was reinforced with bands of metal, and secured with a huge lock.

"That's the Treasure Room," said Ichabod.

"Emperor's orders, nobody is allowed to go in."

"Well?" said Eddy.

Ichabod reached for his keys. He picked out the biggest and heaviest.

"It's this one," he said.

NO ENTRY

PLUCK
AND
PLUCKABILITY

Eddy felt the ruby ring nestling in his pocket. It was the only thing that the Codcakers had taken from the Emperor's treasure store, because the Captain was worried that if they didn't return to *The Codcake* with exactly what the map had ordered – no more, no less – then it might decide they had failed and the whole quest would be over.

Ichabod led them down a long underground passage. After a few minutes, they reached a wooden door. It was thick with spiders' webs and looked like it hadn't been opened for years. A hammer from the Crew's rucksack soon loosened the two rusty bolts that held it shut. Hands tugged at the handle, the hinges let out a complaining creak, and the door swung back.

They all stood bathing in sunlight and fresh air. All that is, except Ichabod, who squinted into the brightness, let out a piercing shriek, and scuttled back underground.

Eddy stepped forward into a forest glade. After the slime and grime of the dungeon, he was just thinking how good it would be to slip his shoes and socks off and feel the grass between his toes, when he heard a familiar voice. It was the Chevalier François Cabernet Lalande-de-Pomerol.

"I should have known you would escape, Captain. That you were only pretending to be helpless to trick them. Did the Emperor squeal like a startled piglet when you attacked?"

"Not quite," said the Captain. "What are you two doing here?"

"We came to rescue you. How foolish to think you would need our help. Still it was nothing – a simple matter of climbing the hundred stairs back up to the castle, disguising ourselves as a pair of glacé cherries, persuading the Emperor's loveliest kitchen maid to smuggle us out of the palace on two iced cupcakes, stealing a map of the forest from the Imperial gamekeeper, discovering the location of the secret back entrance to the dungeons, slipping past the many sharp-toothed creatures of the woods, and then hurling ourselves repeatedly at this door in a noble but painful attempt to break it down."

"You've got real pluck," said the Captain. "All that to rescue us?"

"Of course," said the Chevalier. "You are our comrades."

"It was very brave," said Eddy, realizing that the raisins had not run away and left them at all.

"Better to risk everything than to crawl through life as a coward," said the Chevalier. "Especially if there is a chance to annoy the Emperor – may a dog sneeze on his breakfast. And it was a great plan – bold, daring, inventive, romantic – all except the bit with the door, that really stinks."

"And now you must hurry back to your boat," said Plonque. "The guards may discover that you are gone at any moment."

"It is this way," said the Chevalier. "Take the left fork in the path out of the glade."

⚓ ⚓ ⚓

Eddy thought that he had never seen a sky quite so blue, felt sunshine quite so warm, or smelled blossom quite so blossomy. They had escaped the Emperor and the Beast and the dungeons and they were still alive. They had collected the fourth and last object that the map had sent them to find and they were still alive. They had proved they were worthy to win the treasure and they were still alive.

I feel like skipping, he thought, *but it would look a bit silly*. Then he noticed that the Captain was already skipping, and joined in.

The Codcakers would have felt a lot less happy if they had seen what was happening down the right fork in the path.

A tattered cow costume lay tossed into a bush.

Two men in pink underwear stood tied to two tree trunks.

A hundred hairy sailors circled them, mooing and mocking.

At their centre was Barracuda Bill.

In his raised hand a pair of silver tweezers glinted in the sunlight.

"Hold 'em still, boys," he growled. "These past few days, I kept hearing tales of a strange cow wandering round the islands. But no one could tell me what it was up to. So, I'll ask you two again – are you going to let me in on your secret, or is it time to pluck another nostril?"

The men in pink sobbed.

"I can't take any more," whimpered one.

"We'll tell you why we're here," sobbed the other. "But please put the tweezers down. We're keeping an eye on *The Codcake* while its crew hunt for treasure."

"Treasure! So that's what they're up to," said Barracuda Bill, with a glint in his one good eye. "Then I reckon it's time to pay them another little visit!"

A TRIP TO ROCKY ISLAND

Back on *The Codcake*, the map was being no help at all. Eddy couldn't work it out. They had brought back the ruby ring, just as it had told them to, but all that had appeared on the map was the word "WAIT". *Perhaps it's broken*, Eddy thought. But how did you mend a magic map? You couldn't just stick new batteries in it, or hit the wonky button very gently in just the right place with a hammer like his dad had done that time he cracked the TV screen.

He remembered how much his dad made him laugh. Sometimes it was even on purpose. And how often his mum got the giggles. He had been thinking about them a lot since the Beast almost bit his head off. He wondered what they were doing right now.

"Cheer up!" It was the Crew. "You and the Captain with your long faces."

"I tried to be extra careful," said the Captain. "But I still nearly got us all killed."

"But we're all fine," said the Crew. "Thanks to Eddy's cleverness."

"Ahem," said the Penguin. "Not forgetting the great smell of fish – which stopped us getting chomped by that ugly monster. Fish caught by yours truly."

"We're a team," the Crew added. "Like the raisins said. And we're all right behind you, Captain."

"Thank you, Crew," said the Captain, sounding a bit more cheerful. "But we all needs to keep our wits about us for whatever that map throws at us next."

"It's still not doing anything," said Eddy.

"While we're waiting, let's see a bit of that teamwork," said the Captain. "Pinwing – you're on watch. Crew – mind the map. Cabin Boy – we have unfinished business. I'm not stopping till I'm ahead. So, how many monkeys have I got in my pocket?"

Eddy decided he'd be very happy to give the wrong answer and let the Captain win if it meant the game could end.

"Eleven," he answered quickly.

"Wrong," said the Captain. "The answer is none. Ha, ha! I knew I'd get you eventually."

"Well done," said Eddy. "Now, before we carry on, do you mind if I give you a clue?"

"Go ahead," said the Captain. "All's fair in How Many Monkeys."

"The clue is – I haven't got any monkeys in my pocket." That should get it over with.

"Very cunning," said the Captain. He stroked his beard thoughtfully. Eddy could hear him muttering "bluff" and "double bluff". After a couple of minutes he said, "In fact, it's as cunning as a weasel with dark glasses and a stick-on moustache. But not cunning enough. I've worked it out. I think you think that I'll think that you want me to think that you have no monkeys in your pocket. But I don't think you thought as how I would think you thought that – so I don't think what you thought I'd think you thought I think. In fact, I think I think the opposite. You see?"

"Not really," said Eddy. "You lost me a few thoughts back."

"To put it in a seashell," the Captain continued, "I think you have three monkeys in your pocket. Aha!"

"Uh-uh." Eddy shook his head. "I have no monkeys in my pocket."

"Really?" the Captain asked. "I can't think where I went wrong."

"Tell me, Captain, how many times have you played this game?"

"Hundreds," said the Captain. "Thousands."

"And has anybody ever actually had a monkey in their pocket?"

"Not yet," said the Captain. "But only a fool would think that means there couldn't be a monkey next time."

Eddy was still wondering how that sentence could sound both very sensible and very stupid, when the Crew shouted, "The map has given us our next destination. Rocky Island – and there's a big black cross on the drawing!"

"What about the instructions?" asked the Captain.

"It's writing that now. It says, 'G'... Oh, now it has stopped. 'G.' What kind of instruction is 'G'?"

"'G' for Grungeybeard!" yelled the Captain. "That cross must be where his treasure is buried! Pearls as big as conkers, diamonds as big as gulls' eggs, and emeralds as big as very fat hamsters!"

"Rocky Island is straight ahead on the map," said Eddy excitedly.

"I'll tell the Pinwing to keep a good look out for it," said the Captain.

But at that moment the Penguin called, "Oi! I can see a rocky sort of island thingy!"

"I've told you before," said the Captain, "sailors must shout, 'Land ahoy!'"

"But—"

"No buts. Say it properly and—"

The Captain was silenced by a terrible grinding noise. *The Codcake* suddenly stopped dead, throwing them all off their feet.

"What was that?" said Eddy, picking himself up.

The Penguin's voice drifted down the deck.

"Land ahoy!" he said. "About as ahoy as it could possibly get."

They had found Rocky Island. They clambered down
from the ship, stumbled over rocks draped with
seaweed and pocked with barnacles, and stood back to
inspect their vessel. She was still in one piece, but well
and truly run aground.

"Stranded!" wailed the Captain.
"It's true – the treasure is cursed.
What use are gold and jewels
if we're stuck here?"

"I don't think it's that bad," interrupted Eddy. "Look – the seaweed on the rocks goes way above where *The Codcake* is sitting. And seaweed only grows where there's sea. So the water must get much higher when the tide comes in. I reckon *The Codcake* will just float off when it does."

"I knew that," said the Captain hurriedly. "Course I did. Well done, lad, well spotted, top marks. We'll make a pirate of you yet. Now let's find that treasure. Team – set to!"

The Crew pulled spades from the bag over her shoulder, and handed them round.

"I'll start by that big rock on my left," said the Captain. "Crew, you try the right, over by that other rock. Pinwing – you start at that rock near *The Codcake*, and Eddy try round that little rock sticking up over there."

"Actually," said Eddy, "if you don't mind, I might try digging right here. I've got a funny feeling about this spot."

He pointed towards his feet. He was standing right in the middle of a huge black cross that had been painted on the ground.

X MARKS THE WHAT?

With a shout, they all started digging into the cross. Three spades bit the ground, while the Penguin scuffed at it with his feet, throwing sand and rocks behind him in a great plume. They worked deeper and deeper until, with a loud CLUNK, the Crew hit something solid.

They scrabbled with hands and flippers to clear what they soon saw was a large wooden chest. It had a small copper plate on its lid. Salt and sand had eaten at it, but Eddy could still read out the words that were engraved on it – LOOK INSIDE.

The Captain stood back, panting with the effort.

"Grungeybeard's treasure chest! I wants to savour this moment," he said. "We are going to be rich beyond our wildest dreams."

"Are you sure about that?" said the Penguin. "Because when it comes to being rich, my dreams get very wild indeed."

They heaved at the lid and it slowly began to move.

"This is it!" shouted the Captain, and with one last tug they forced the chest wide open. They peered excitedly inside. But instead of heaps of gold and precious stones, the sunlight fell on a small, dull, brown brick.

"Dodgy bottom!" shouted the Captain.

"This is no time to discuss your medical problems," said the Penguin.

"No," said the Captain. "I mean the chest must have a dodgy bottom, with a secret compartment underneath it where the treasure is hidden!"

He tossed the brick over his shoulder, and smashed at the bottom of the chest with his spade. After a few lusty blows, the wood began to splinter. And suddenly, they could all see…sand.

"Real bottom," said the Penguin.

"I don't understand," said the Captain. "Where's

Grungeybeard's treasure?"

"Hang on a minute," said Eddy. "Where's that brick?"

He picked it up and sniffed it. It had a familiar smell. Where had he smelled that before?

Oh, no. He felt a sinking feeling in his stomach.

"Captain," he said, "remind me. How did you know we were on Grungeybeard's trail?"

"It was my dream," said the Captain. "I saw his name written across the sky."

"And how was it spelled?"

"I remember there were two 'guhs' and a 'nuh' and a 'ruh' at the start," said the Captain. "And a 'buh' and a 'ruh' and a 'duh'."

"I see," said Eddy. "Grungeybeard has all those letters. But so does…gingerbread." He held up the dull, brown brick. "The word you saw in the sky wasn't *Grungeybeard*. It was *gingerbread*."

The Captain shuffled uncomfortably from one foot to the other.

"Ooh," he said. "Ahhh."

"The map was never leading us to treasure," Eddy said sadly.

"Oh, dear," said the Crew. "That is a bit disappointing.

215

Still, at least we had a lovely adventure."

"Why do you always have to look on the bright side?" said the Penguin. "It's really depressing."

"It could be worse," said the Captain. He was blushing bright pink. "I mean…oh, I don't know what I mean. And it couldn't be worse. I don't even like gingerbread."

"Somebody must have a very strange sense of humour," said the Crew. "To make the magic map and work out the tasks and bury this chest. It's a lot of effort for a bit of cake."

"You're right," said Eddy. "That's very odd. Unless we're missing something."

"Like what?" said the Crew. "The sign said look inside. And we did."

"Maybe we haven't looked at the right inside," said Eddy. "I wonder." He threw the gingerbread brick on the ground, took a spade, and whacked it as hard as he could.

The gingerbread shattered into a billion crumbs. And one other thing.

"Look!" said Eddy. "There was a piece of paper baked into it."

He picked it up. There was writing on it. Neat, round, old-fashioned handwriting.

"This must be what we were meant to find," said Eddy, smoothing out the paper and brushing off the crumbs. "It's a poem."

AT LAST! You've found the final clue
Brave traveller on your quest.
Now get back on your ship at ONCE
And sail twelve miles due west.
There you will find an island where
A GREAT reward is waiting.
Do as you're TOLD! SHUT UP! Sit STILL!
I hope you're concentrating!
Bring all your loot – the chocolates, poem,
Ruby ring and flowers
And find a gorgeous palace
With one thousand and one towers.
Got that? Then MOVE IT! Hurry up!
I will NOT tell you twice.
It's time to claim what you have won –
A TREASURE BEYOND PRICE.

"A treasure beyond price," repeated the Captain. "I likes the sound of that."

"Me too," said Eddy. "That's a lot more than we'll need to save Gran's cottage. The poem is very bossy, though."

"Never mind that. Grungeybeard or no Grungeybeard, I reckons this is all going to turn out just right."

"Why did you have to say that?" said the Penguin. "It's asking for everything to go just wrong."

"Stop being such a misery," said the Captain.

BOOM BOOM

What we doing?

"Did you hear something?" asked Eddy.

BOOM BOOM

Where we going?

"No," said the Captain.

BOOM BOOM

Are we there yet?

"Oh," said the Captain.

"What did I tell you?" said the Penguin.

"Perhaps they won't spot us," said the Crew. "Perhaps they won't bother with us if they do."

"Cooooooeeeeeee! Little *Codcake*!" Barracuda Bill bellowed. "I be a-coming to get you!"

"You were saying?" said the Penguin.

EVERYBODY
DIES

"Right," said the Captain. "It's very important for everybody to *STAY CALM!!!!!!!!!!!!!*"

"You just have a nice sit down, dearie, and try to stop shaking," the Crew said to the Captain. "I survived the Great Freeze of '63, the Great Flood of '74, and the Great Toilet Paper Shortage of '82. I can get through this, too. We've just got to consider all the options."

"We can't run away," said Eddy, "because the ship has run aground. We can't hide, because we're standing on a big bare rock. We can't fight, because we can't fight."

"Let's face it," said the Penguin. "If Barracuda Bill attacks, we're doomed."

"Which means," said the Crew, "we've got to find a way to stop him attacking in the first place."

"Maybe we can frighten him off," said Eddy. "What if we were sick? I read in my *Big Book of Ships* that pirates were terrified of deadly diseases getting on board."

"So your plan for survival is for us to catch a fatal illness," said the Penguin. "I think I can see a tiny flaw."

"We don't have to catch it," said Eddy. "We just have to make them believe we've caught it. My book has a picture of a ship flying a big yellow flag to warn other vessels to keep clear. So, we need something big and yellow."

"Auntie's painting!" shouted the Crew. "It's got a few purple splodges where the Taj Mahal's meant to be, but they'll hardly show from a distance."

"Great!" said Eddy. "Get it from the Captain's cabin and we'll run it up the flagpole. And then we have to put on a show to convince the pirates. We need someone who can act. Penguin – I think this is your big moment."

⚓ ⚓ ⚓

The Captain was draped over the ship's wheel, playing dead. The Crew lay sprawled across the deck. Eddy was flat out nearby, eyes shut, his tongue lolling out of his mouth.

"Boarding party, prepare grappling irons!" Barracuda Bill's voice was alarmingly close.

Eddy opened one eyelid the tiniest fraction, and peeped out. *The Scavenger* was almost alongside. And two dozen of the biggest, hairiest, bristling-with-weaponsiest pirates that you could ever wish not to meet were lined up at the ready.

Perhaps their plan wasn't going to work.

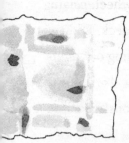

"Boarding party, swing grappling irons!"

They were coming. And there was nowhere to run.

"Yellow Jack!" a voice suddenly yelled. At last, someone had spotted the warning flag.

Another shouted, "They'm got fever aboard!" and "Hold, lads!" and there was a jostling and muttering and "I see a body!" and "There's another!" and the clunking of grappling irons as they were dropped to the deck.

It's working, thought Eddy. He could hear the alarm in their voices.

But then Barracuda Bill growled, "Are you lily-livered chicken-hearted milk-swigging lackguts going to fall for that old trick? I reckon if one of those bodies feels your boot you'll soon find out they're as alive as you or me. And there's a ducat in my pocket for the man who'll prove me right."

Then the muttering changed in tone, and one particularly big, particularly hairy, particularly bristling-with-weaponsy pirate stepped forward and shouted, "I say the Captain's right! I'll win that ducat, and crack a few bones while I'm about it. Stand back, boys, and let me at 'em."

Oh, no, thought Eddy. *We're done for.*

And then from behind him he heard a pitiful groan and a hacking cough and the Penguin stumbled across his view.

"Dead!" wailed the Penguin. "All dead – and me not long for this world neither! Ohhhhh! Why me? I'm too young and handsome and just plain all-round brilliant to die!"

He tottered around the deck, then raised a feeble

flipper towards *The Scavenger*, a look of terror on his face.

"Ohhhhhh! It's the fever – the terrible fever – it's Poor Sore Head. Stay back, or it will kill all of you, too."

He cried out twice, a cry that was no more than a breath – "The horror! The horror!" And then with a final twirl on one foot, he collapsed, limp and silent.

On board *The Scavenger*, there wasn't a sound, not even a whisper – until the noise of a carelessly dropped pin shattered the mood.

"It looks like they really are ill," said Barracuda Bill. "Let's get out of here."

We're safe, thought Eddy. *Well done, Penguin!*

But then:

"And now, ladies and gentlemen…"

It was the Penguin. *What!?*

"What do you give to a fish with no ears?"

"You stupid bird!" And now the Captain spoke. "You've ruined everything."

Oh, no.

With a snarl and a roar and a whirling of grappling irons, a blur of pirates swung from deck to deck.

"I had to go for an encore," said the Penguin. "The audience were mine – completely enthralled. It's every performer's dream."

"And here," said the Captain, "comes every sailor's nightmare."

Barracuda Bill! A balding parrot sitting on his shoulder screeched, "Time for bye-byes!" and then chuckled cruelly. Bill bent forward and thrust his face so close that Eddy could see the fleas jumping in his bristling red beard. He opened his lips, revealing a mouthful of long, sharp teeth.

"What ho, me hearties?" he growled.

PARROT AND CARROT

"Who shall we begin with, then?" said Barracuda Bill. "Small boy, old lady, weird black and white duck, or little pirate?" He frowned at the Captain. "Do you know you've got a carrot on your shoulder?"

"And you've got parrot poo all down your back," said the Captain, as the parrot plopped a big one on Barracuda Bill's coat, and squawked, "Polly wants a nut!"

"Ouch!" replied Barracuda Bill, as the grumpy parrot sank its beak into his earlobe.

"I'm not a duck," the Penguin began.

"If I say you're a duck, you're a duck," snarled Barracuda Bill. "Understand?"

"Quack!" said the Penguin.

"I heard that you lot have been collecting treasure," said Barracuda Bill. "Now, we can do this the hard way, or the easy way."

"Easy way, please. Quack!" said the Penguin.

"Just joking – I only do the hard way. Can you guess how I'm going to make you tell me where your treasure is hidden?"

Before he could reveal what horrible plan he had in mind, the door to the Captain's cabin burst open, and two burly pirates staggered on deck carrying his sea chest.

"We've found it, skipper," one of them said cheerfully.

Barracuda Bill didn't look pleased.

"Oh, bilge rats!" he shouted. "I haven't even started playing with this lot and up you pops with their treasure chest. Where's the fun in that?"

"Sorry, skipper," said the first pirate.

"We got this, too," said the second pirate, pulling the silent warbleflower from his pocket. "We could always hide the chest again, and then you could try to find it."

"No, no," said Barracuda Bill, "the moment's gone.

It just wouldn't be the same. Still, let's see what they've collected." He swung his cutlass and snapped both the padlocks on the chest with one blow, then rummaged through the contents.

"The ruby ring's not bad but the rest is rubbish. Still, what can you expect from a bunch of amateurs?"

And then he spotted the piece of paper that they had found in the gingerbread. It was poking out of Eddy's shirt pocket – but not for long.

"Aha!" said Barracuda Bill as he unfolded it, and, "Oho!" as he read the verse. "That will do very nicely. A treasure beyond price. Not such rubbish after all, then. I'll take this bit of paper – and the rest."

"That's not fair!" said Eddy. "We did all the hard work, and now you're just going to steal it from us!"

"Talk to the hook," said Barracuda Bill.

"But we need it," said Eddy, "to save my gran's cottage from falling down."

"You're wasting your breath," said Barracuda Bill. "I've heard them all before. We need new sails. The orphanage roof wants mending. My puppy's got a sore paw. Heard them, ignored them, had a good laugh about them later."

"You always were a rotter," said the Captain.

"Oh! Hello! It's the little pirate. And what do you know?"

"He knows a lot," said Eddy, "and he's not a little pirate, he's…"

"Don't," said the Captain.

"…the famous Captain Jake McHake."

"You did," groaned the Captain.

"McHake?" said Barracuda Bill. "That name rings a bell. I've met a McHake before. But he wasn't a Captain. McHake? Who was he…? Oh, I remember now. He was a shop assistant in a dump of a place called Pirate Cove. He was a right blunderhead. Couldn't even read the customers' orders properly. I once asked for salted herrings and got assorted earrings. You'd write down 'cutlasses', and end up with cutlets. Instead of a sack of parrot feed, he sent me a pack of carrot seed. I wonder what happened to that clown…hang on a minute! Parrot… Carrot."

He stared at the orange vegetable on the Captain's shoulder with his one good eye. Then he lifted his eyepatch and stared with his one bad eye as well.

"It's you, isn't it? And you thought that a miserable

mollusc like yourself could be a Captain? No wonder you're sailing such a tatty old ship. No wonder it's ended up halfway up this rock. No wonder you could only get this ragbag rabble to follow you."

The Captain looked down at his boots.

"You're no pirate, McHake. You're just a fake." Barracuada Bill laughed a fruity laugh. Then he stuffed the warbleflower in his pocket, stuck the paper between his teeth, hooked hold of the treasure chest, grabbed a rope and swung himself back aboard his own ship – followed by the rest of his boarding party.

The Codcakers gloomily watched them sail –

BOOM
BOOM

– into the distance.

"That went better than I expected," said the Penguin.

Eddy had to ask the question – though he really didn't want to hear the answer.

"Is it true?" he said. "Are you really not a pirate?"

"I stood behind the counter in that shop for years," said the Captain. "I used to see all the sea dogs coming in with their tales of exotic islands and fabulous treasures and thrilling adventures. Not that they ever talked to me, of course. I was just the nobody in the corner. I used to dream of setting sail like them. And then one night I had a dream that I *could* set sail like them and the next morning I woke up in your bath and the rest you know."

"So you are a fake," said Eddy sadly.

"McHake the Fake," the Captain mumbled. "Yes, that's me."

"But I believed in you. I believed we were going to find the loot and save my gran's cottage! Well, stupid me for being fooled, because that's not going to happen is it, Captain McFake?"

"No," said the Captain. "It's not."

Eddy felt his stomach churning. An hour ago he had been a member of a pirate crew on the trail of treasure. Now he was face-to-face with a fraud in fancy dress and the treasure was sailing off over the horizon in the clutches of a vicious maniac. The whole trip had been a huge waste of time and now it was over.

"I feel like someone's torn my dreams into shreds and dropped them in a puddle and jumped up and down on them in wellington boots until they're all just so much mashed-up mush. You promised you would teach me to be a pirate, but you hadn't even got the first idea how to do it yourself. All you can do is wear your stupid carrot and lead us into trouble!"

He stomped away across the deck of the stranded *Codcake*.

"That's too harsh," the Crew called after him.

"No, it's not," said the Captain. "I deserve everything he's said. I've let him down. He believed in me. No one has ever done that before. But I pretended to be something that I'm not."

"You once told me that at sea you can be anyone you want to be," said the Crew. "Look at me – back in Tidemark Bay I'm just the timid old lady who runs the junk shop. Out here I'm the Crew, facing whatever comes our way. Who cares who you were back onshore? Right now you've got a ship and a treasure map and a dream to follow. What more do you need to be a pirate? But if you want Eddy to believe in you, you have to believe in yourself first."

"I almost did," said the Captain. "When it started. But it all got so difficult. And dangerous. And I couldn't get anything right."

"And yet we are all still here. The only people who never make mistakes are the ones who never try anything. And what sort of life is that? A life that hides in its miserable little hole. So buck up! This is what you are now – Captain of *The Codcake*. And if you want to wear a carrot on your shoulder, you wear a carrot on your shoulder – and be sure to wear it proudly."

"Do you really think I can do it?" said the Captain.

"Do *you* really think you can do it?" answered the Crew.

The Captain looked out across the sea for a moment. Then he straightened the carrot, puffed out his chest and shouted, "Cabin boy!" Eddy turned. "We are not going to let Barracuda Bill get away with this. I am going to stand up to him."

"Hold on a minute," said the Penguin. "Are you sure this is sensible?"

"No," said the Captain. "I'm sure this is not sensible. Sensible is a shop assistant being bossed around and ignored. But since when was a pirate captain sensible? What was it the raisins said? Better to risk everything than to crawl through life as a coward."

"He'll mash you," said the Penguin, "into teeny tiny bits."

"I don't want you to get hurt," said Eddy. "Even if you are a fake."

"Then you had better come with me. I reckons we'll need your brains if we're going to have a chance to get that treasure and save your gran's cottage like I promised."

Eddy thought about how Barracuda Bill had sneered at them. Why should he be allowed to steal everything that they had worked for? The four of them had beaten all the other challenges on the way – maybe they could work out a way to beat this one as well.

"Okay," he said, "I'm in."

"That's the spirit."

"But that doesn't mean everything is all right again."

"Understood," said the Captain. "As soon as the tide floats us off this rock, we are sailing twelve miles due west. I just needs to work out what to do when we gets there."

TWELVE MILES DUE WEST

"A palace with one thousand and one towers," said the Captain. "That's what the rhyme said we had to find. Shouldn't be hard to spot."

Twelve miles due west from Rocky Island, the Codcakers had found land. They had boarded their

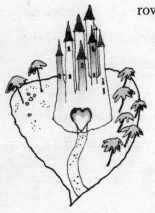

rowing boat and beached it on the secluded shoreline. Right now all that they could spot was sand and palm trees. A lot of palm trees.

"Wait here while I see if I can find a way through," said the Captain, disappearing into the greenery.

"He's very unhappy, you know," the Crew said to Eddy. "He feels that he's let you down."

"He has let me down. He's let us all down. Since we set sail, what has he done – apart from blunder around?"

"I'll tell you what he has done, dearie. His best. And that's all you can ask of anyone."

"But why did he have to make up all the stuff about being a pirate?"

The Crew let out a long sigh. "I think he just got carried away. He started telling the story about the person he wished he was because he liked it more than the reality. It's not unusual, you know, dearie. Maybe it will never happen to you. Maybe you will never be tempted to say things about yourself that are a bit more than true. Maybe everything in your life will work out just as you planned and you'll always be the person you want to be. But if so, you'll be one in a million."

"Things are already wrong in my life," said Eddy. "My parents sent me to Tidemark Bay for a summer of fresh air and fun because they are too busy to have me around."

"Do you think that's how they wanted their lives to turn out? Being too busy? I bet they are doing their best, too. Most people do. Even when they get things wrong. Right now the Captain is doing his best to work out how to stand up to that horrible Barracuda Bill. If he gets that wrong things could get very nasty indeed. So he needs you on his side again."

They heard the Captain crashing back towards them through the undergrowth.

"Blasted blithering trees!" his voice boomed out. Then the crashing suddenly stopped and he spoke more quietly.

"Hello, what's this? Well, well, well."

A moment later he stepped back onto the sand. He was fiddling with the flap on one of his pockets.

"Did you find a path?" asked the Crew.

"No," said the Captain. "That jungle's a right jumble."

"Would you kindly follow me?" The voice belonged to a distinguished grey-haired figure who emerged from the trees. He wore a friendly smile and a startlingly pink suit. On each side of him stood a companion, of similar age and similarly dressed.

"We are here to guide you to the end of your long quest."

"You knows about our quest?" asked the Captain.

"We do. Ever since the map was activated our cow-disguised intelligence unit have been watching you – although we have lost touch with them recently. We've been expecting you Captain McHake – and, of course, Crew, Eddy and Penguin."

"And who are you?" asked the Captain.

"My name is not important."

"All the same," answered the Captain, "we'd like to know who you are."

"But I've already told you." The man smiled. "I'm Not Important."

The figure to his right spoke up. "That's right, he's called Not Important, I'm Who Asked You In The First Place, and this is Shut Up And Get On With Your Work. She gives us all names like that."

"And who is She?" asked Eddy.

"Why, Beautiful Princess Ermintrelda, of course," said Shut Up.

"So is this princess in charge round here?" asked the Captain.

239

"Beautiful Princess Ermintrelda? Indeed so," answered Not Important.

"In charge of the treasure beyond price and all that?"

"Oh, yes. And she will meet you at the palace. This way, please."

Not Important led the Codcakers along the beach to a gap in the trees.

"Have you decided what to do when we get there?" the Crew whispered to the Captain.

"Not yet." He tapped his forehead. "I'm working on it. I just hope I hurry up."

The gap turned into a path that climbed steadily until it opened onto a wide grassy hillside. A vast palace stood in the valley below, its dazzling white walls shining out against green fields in the afternoon sunlight. Dozens of towers rose and branched out into ever more turrets and points and pinnacles, too many to count. Topped with slanted roofs of coloured tiles, and fluttering with bright flags and pennants, they bristled against the sky.

"Wow," said Eddy. "That's amazing."

"Beautiful," said the Crew.

"Beautiful!" shouted the Captain. "That's it! I've

worked out what to do. We're meeting a beautiful princess, right? Well, everyone knows that beautiful princesses are always kind and good. It's part of the job. So I reckons that if I tell her that we did the quest but Barracuda Bill stole everything from us, she is bound to decide to give the treasure to us."

"Has he arrived yet?" Eddy asked Not Important. "Barracuda Bill, I mean?"

"I know nothing of a Mister Bill," said Not Important.

"Life's better that way. Enjoy it while you still can," said the Penguin.

They walked down the hillside and halted outside the palace gates.

"Before we enter," said Not Important, "it is my duty to inform you of certain rules which must be followed. All weapons are to be surrendered. You are to behave politely and peacefully when in the presence of Beautiful Princess Ermintrelda. If you misbehave you will be barred from the quest for the treasure beyond price. Is that clear?"

"As a rock pool," said the Captain.

"Then please follow me."

They passed through the gates and entered a broad courtyard. A huge pile of swords, muskets, pistols, knives and other generally hurty objects lay just inside. The Captain threw his sword onto the heap, and followed the rest of the party into the palace and up a wide marble staircase.

At the top, Eddy found himself staring at a life-sized portrait of the most beautiful woman that he had ever seen. She wore a long, white gown, and was holding out her right hand as though to beckon them into her presence. Tumbling ringlets of jet-black hair framed a perfectly proportioned face, her eyes dazzlingly blue, her nose pert, her lips full and red. A dozen young men were pictured sprawling adoringly around her feet.

"Cor," said the Captain.

"I like her frock," said the Crew.

"Is that Beautiful Princess Ermintrelda?" asked Eddy.

"No," said Not Important. "That is a painting of Beautiful Princess Ermintrelda. Beautiful Princess Ermintrelda will meet you in her private apartments. This way."

He led the Codcakers down a long corridor to a tall

double door, which opened onto a room that was pink from floor to ceiling – shaggy pink carpet under their feet, pink flowery paper on the walls, pink silk curtains over the windows, pink striped armchairs and a pink polka-dotted sofa. There was even a pink chandelier hanging above their heads. In fact, just about the only things in the room that weren't completely pink were the seated figures of Barracuda Bill and two of his crew.

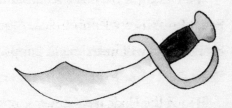

MEET THE PRINCESS

"What are these losers doing here?" said Barracuda Bill, rising from his seat.

"I take it you've already met," said a voice from across the room. Eddy turned to see another pink-suited figure. "I'm Something I Trod In, by the way. And this charming gentleman," he explained to Not Important, "is Barracuda Bill, with his colleagues Bonecrusher Bert and Jellyfish Jones."

"We calls him Jellyfish," said Barracuda Bill, "because—"

"Please," interrupted Something I Trod In. "They don't want to know. You told me an hour ago and I'm still feeling sick."

"Are you going to give me this treasure beyond price soon, or am I going to have to start breaking things?" said Barracuda Bill. "Or people?" he added with a snarl.

"Manners, please," said Something I Trod In. "Or there will be no treasure for you. Remember the rules."

"I hate rules," said Barracuda Bill. But he sat down again.

"Typical, isn't it?" said Something I Trod In. "We wait years for someone to come to claim the treasure beyond price, and then two turn up at once. No planning."

"And no Beautiful Princess Ermintrelda?" asked Not Important.

"She's with Maintenance," said Something I Trod In. "Hair failure."

"Her hair looked lovely in her portrait," said Eddy.

"*She* looked lovely in her portrait," said the Captain.

"Pah!" said Barracuda Bill. "I saw that daub. What a soppy, floppy, prissy miss. And those drippy lads lying round like limp litter…"

A door on the far side of the room rattled open. With cries of "Heave!" and a sudden FFFFLLLLOOOOOFFFF! a great billow of white silk squeezed through the doorway and erupted into the room. It rippled and ruffled as it was carried forward by pink-uniformed servants. Something inside the white mass was screeching. An arm emerged, and a hand slapped the nearest servant across the back of his head, and then began waving regally.

The billow settled into the shape of a dress, its edges yellowing and tattered. A head suddenly came into view, like a swimmer bobbing in a foamy sea – a female head, as faded and frayed as her dress. Her dark hair shot off at unlikely angles, like a small explosion in a wig factory. Bright pink lipstick blotched from her mouth onto her patchily powdered cheek. A false eyelash wandered towards her right ear. The whole effect was of someone who had been dragged through a hedge backwards. And then forwards, to make sure they were thoroughly messed up. And then backwards again just for the fun of it.

"Pray be upstanding," said Not Important, "for Beautiful Princess Ermintrelda!"

"That's the Princess?" said Eddy. "Blimey!"

"Blimey!" said the Captain.

"Blimey!" said Barracuda Bill, his mouth hanging open.

"Brave adventurers!" Beautiful Princess Ermintrelda flumped down onto the sofa. "Get on with it!"

Not Important stepped forward.

"Beautiful Princess Ermintrelda will now receive the four items that you have collected to prove yourselves worthy to win the treasure without price.

Four tokens of your courage, ingenuity, fortit—"

"Blah! Blah! Blah!" Beautiful Princess Ermintrelda interrupted him. "Come on, hand over the stuff. Flowers first."

Barracuda Bill fished into a sack and pulled out the little plant – which immediately began to sing.

"LA-LA-LA-LA-LA," it trilled merrily.

"How charming," said Beautiful Princess Ermintrelda.

"LA-LA-LA-LA-LA-LA-LA-LA-LA-LA-LA-LA-LAAAAAAAAAAA-LA."

"Delightful. And now…"

"LA-LI-LOO-LI-OOBY-DOOBY-LIBBIDY-LOBBIDY-LOO-LA."

"Someone tell that plant that if it doesn't shut up it will soon be compost!"

"LA-LI-*erk!*" The plant ended its performance with a strangled yelp.

"One warbleflower from Barracuda Bill." Beautiful Princess Ermintrelda turned to the Captain. "Where's yours, then?"

"I… Er…" said the Captain, struggling to find the right words. She didn't seem to be the kind and good princess that he had been expecting. "Um…"

"That warbleflower is ours," said Eddy.

"No, no, no," said Beautiful Princess Ermintrelda. "I saw Barracuda Bill take it out of his bag."

"But…" the Captain spluttered.

"I understand," said Beautiful Princess Ermintrelda. "My beauty has left you speechless. It happens all the time. So much so, that people say that being this gorgeous must be a burden. But I say nuts to that, because it means I get loads of prezzies. Poem next. Come on!"

"Got it." Barracuda Bill pulled a bright green leaf from his pocket – the bright green leaf that the Captain had been given by the Poet Tree. The bright green leaf in which the Poet Tree had expressed all the secret longings that the Captain had whispered to it. Bill began to read aloud:

"Oh! The pirate life is thrilling
And the lads are bold and gruff
They do pillaging and stealing
And other rough tough stuff.
But a pirate can get thinking
And a pirate can get glum
For there's more to life than fighting,
Treasure, yo-ho-ho and rum…"

Eddy saw the Captain blush bright red with embarrassment as Bill recited verses that revealed how much the Captain longed for a companion.

"I have heard the mermaids murmur
But a mermaid's half a fish
And I want a girl with legs and not
A scaly tail to swish..."

The Captain flushed even brighter red with anger as Bill recited verses that the Captain had meant to be heard only by his true love – whoever she might turn out to be.

"Will you say you'll be my sweetheart?
Will you end my misery?
It's the tears of lonely sailors
That turn all the seas salty."

Beautiful Princess Ermintrelda suddenly burst into loud sobs. "I've always wanted someone to write me a poem," she wailed.

"And that poem's mine, too," said the Captain, finding his voice. But neither Beautiful Princess Ermintrelda nor Barracuda Bill paid any attention to him.

"So much emotion," Beautiful Princess Ermintrelda sniffled.

"Strangest thing," said Barracuda Bill. "I never felt feelings like the feelings I'm feeling now. It's like something's flapping round in my stomach."

"I often get that," said the Penguin. "It's called fish."

"A life without love is so tragic," blubbed Beautiful Princess Ermintrelda, "as I know only too well." There were tears running down her cheeks, and a long string of snot dangling from her nose.

"Perhaps it's time for that to change," said Barracuda Bill. And he tried a smile. It came out all lopsided and showed a lot of very sharp teeth, but for someone who had never done it before, it really wasn't a bad attempt and only looked a little bit terrifying.

"I do believe," said the Crew, "that there's romance in the air."

Beautiful Princess Ermintrelda yanked at Not Important's jacket and blew her nose loudly on it.

"I think it's time for you to tell me how spectacularly lovely I am," said Beautiful Princess Ermintrelda. "Speak slowly and clearly and pay particular attention to my dainty little nosey and dazzlingly blue eyes."

"Before you two carry on," said the Captain, "we needs to talk about the quest."

"Our quest," Eddy added. "And the things that *we* collected."

"Oh! The rest of my goodies!" said Beautiful Princess Ermintrelda. "Who's got my choccies?"

Barracuda Bill brandished the box of Lanceling Ploverdew's finest creations. Beautiful Princess Ermintrelda grabbed a handful and stuffed them between her lips.

"And the jewel?" she mumbled through a half-chewed mouthful.

Barracuda Bill fished the ruby ring from his sack.

"You win," said Beautiful Princess Ermintrelda. A thread of brown drool dribbled from the corner of her mouth. "Nice chocs, by the way."

"You heard the lady," Barracuda Bill barked.

"But—" said the Captain.

"No," said Eddy. "This isn't right."

"I won," said Bill. "You lost. And now I claim my prize – the treasure beyond price."

THE TREASURE BEYOND PRICE

The Captain took a deep breath. "Objection!"

"Overruled," said Barracuda Bill.

"You haven't even heard what it is yet," said the Captain.

"Don't care," said Barracuda Bill.

"But you cheated," said Eddy. "You didn't do the quest. You just pinched everything from us."

"'You cheated!'" mocked Barracuda Bill. "Of course I cheated. We're pirates, for badness' sake. We steal stuff."

"Beautiful Princess Ermintrelda," said the Captain. "You heard Barracuda Bill. We completed the quest,

253

not him. Does he deserve the treasure beyond price? Do you want to reward meanness and thieving and general all-round horribleness?"

He whipped off his hat, threw out his arm and struck the noblest pose he could muster.

"By all that's decent and true, we Codcakers battled bravely and sweated and strived or stroved or whatever the right word is, and we did it fairly and honourably and it's us what deserves the treasure beyond price, and no mistake!"

"Bravo!" said the Crew.

Eddy had never seen the Captain like this before. His eyes blazed with passion. He seemed to have grown a head taller, and with his chest thrust out he looked as though he had been pumped up with air.

"You did it," said Eddy to the Captain. "You really did it. You stood up to him."

"Standing up is one thing," said the Captain. "But we ain't won that treasure yet."

"Just wondering," said the Penguin. "What exactly is the treasure beyond price?"

"You're looking at it, silly," said Beautiful Princess Ermintrelda. "It's me. That's why I sent out the magic map all those years ago. The winner gets to marry me."

"Ah," said the Captain, suddenly deflating. "Um. Nevertheless. Er – fair play and honour and stuff and, well, you know." His voice trailed away in a hesitant mumble.

"You don't actually want to marry her, do you?" asked Eddy.

"Have a care, boy," said Barracuda Bill. "You're speaking about my girl."

"But she's selfish and bossy and greedy and shouty," said Eddy, "and she calls people horrible names and hits them."

"Yeah! What a woman!" sighed Barracuda Bill. "What's not to love?"

"Love?" squealed Beautiful Princess Ermintrelda. "Why, this is all so sudden!"

"You, my dear, are truly a treasure beyond price – far more special than gold and silver and sapphires and diamonds," said Bill, reaching for her hand.

"I certainly am," said Beautiful Princess Ermintrelda. "For a start, there's only one of me. But there is simply loads of gold and silver. The royal treasury is heaped with it. And don't get me started on all the sapphires and diamonds and rubies that are cluttering up the place. They are such a bore. I can hardly wait to get married so I can hand the whole lot over to my husband."

"To your husband…?" said the Captain. Suddenly marrying the Princess didn't seem an unbearable prospect after all. "Then by all that's fair and decent…"

"We heard you the first time," said Barracuda Bill with a triumphant grin. "You lost. I won. I get the treasure. You get over it."

"This ain't working," the Captain hissed to Eddy. "I don't understand. I had the dream. We discovered the map. I was sure that treasure wanted to be found by us because you need a fortune to fix your gran's cottage."

"Maybe it just wanted to be found," said Eddy, "and it didn't care who found it. Maybe this was really Barracuda Bill's story all along."

"No," said the Captain. "It's our story, and I'm not going to give it up without a fight."

"A fight? You don't mean with Bill?" said Eddy. "He'll kill you."

"Not if the story is meant to be."

"No," said Eddy. "You've done enough. I'm sorry for

all that stuff I said before – and I take it all back. You came after Barracuda Bill and stood up to him like a real pirate. You've proved who you are. You did your best and no one can ask more than that."

"I can," said the Captain. "And I do. I want to win." He tapped Barracuda Bill on the shoulder.

"Coward," said the Captain.

The smile on Barracuda Bill's lips sank into a snarl. A vein on his forehead started to throb.

"He's done it now," said Bonecrusher Bert quietly, as he and Jellyfish Jones sneaked behind the sofa for cover.

Barracuda Bill pushed his face right into the Captain's.

"What – did – you – just – call – me?" he spat.

"C-c-coward," said the Captain, his voice trembling. "You were too scared to do the quest yourself. And now I bet you are too scared to fight for your prize."

"Scared!" roared Barracuda Bill. "Me, scared of a snivelling spineless seaslug like you? I'll show you who's scared!"

He took a glove from his belt, and slapped the Captain across the face with it. Once. Twice.

"Ow. Ow," said the Captain.

"I challenge you to a duel! Man against mollusc!"

"Oh!" squealed Beautiful Princess Ermintrelda. "You boys! Fighting over me!" She bobbed up and down in her chair with excitement. "No, no, no, no, no! You mustn't! You simply simply mustn't! But if you simply simply must you'd better go outside. And don't start till I get there – I don't want to miss a single moment!"

"Outside," said Barracuda Bill. "Now." He stamped away.

"You don't have to go through with this," Eddy said to the Captain. "We won't think any the less of you. Like you once said, there's a difference between courage and stupidity. He's the most dangerous pirate afloat."

"Maybe," said the Captain. "But I have a plan."

"Did you think it up yourself?" said the Penguin.

"Absolutely," said the Captain.

"So," asked the Penguin, "would you like to be buried on land or at sea?"

34

HOW
WOULD YOU
<u>LIKE</u> TO BE
KILLED?

"Coooeeeeee, boys!" Eddy looked up from the palace
courtyard to the balcony where Beautiful Princess
Ermintrelda stood waving and shouting. Beside her,
Not Important raised a megaphone to his lips and
addressed the crowd.

"Your Majesty, My Lords, Ladies and Gentlemen,
Knights, Squires, Peasants, Paupers, Palace Servants
and Scum of the Seven Seas – welcome to this duel for
the hand of Beautiful Princess Ermintrelda. On my left,
the Challenger – Barracuda Bill…"

The crew of *The Scavenger* started to yell and stamp enthusiastically. It was a frightful racket. Not Important waited for it to die down before continuing.

"...And on my right, the Challenged – Captain Jake McHake."

"Hurray!" shouted Eddy, the Penguin and the Crew. But their voices were drowned out by chants of "Fake! Fake! Fake!" from the other side.

"According to the rules of duelling," Not Important continued, "the Challenged will choose the manner of the contest."

Barracuda Bill was standing by the huge pile of discarded weapons near the palace gate. He called to the Captain, "There's pistols, muskets, matchlocks, flintlocks, clubs, cudgels, axes, maces, longbows, crossbows, slingshots, blowpipes, harpoons, cannon, pikes, lances, longswords, shortswords, sortofinbetweenswords and even a rare set of razor-edged fighting antlers. So, you decide. Do you want to be sliced, diced, slashed, bashed, stabbed, hacked, pierced, pummelled, blasted, bludgeoned, poisoned, shot or butted to death?"

The Captain walked slowly up to Barracuda Bill to look him straight in the eyes – although, as he was a good deal shorter than his opponent he only managed to look him straight in the beard.

"I choose…" And he paused.

The air bristled with tension. Eddy could hardly stand it.

"……………" paused the Captain.

"Get on with it," shouted someone in the crowd.

"I choose – a match of How Many Monkeys Have I Got In My Pocket?"

"Ha!" Barracuda Bill snorted into the Captain's hat. "You chose the wrong game, pipsqueak. In all the Seven Seas, no one has ever beaten me at How Many Monkeys Have I Got In My Pocket? I'm going to enjoy this."

"The Captain is terrible at How Many Monkeys," said Eddy.

"Goodbye, treasure," said the Penguin.

"But at least he won't be sliced or diced or meet any other horrible end," said the Crew.

"And afterwards," said Barracuda Bill, "I can have fun trying out some of these lovely weapons on you."

"Ah," said the Crew.

The Captain marked out twenty paces and turned back to face Barracuda Bill.

"Game on!" he shouted at his opponent.

Barracuda Bill's voice thundered across the courtyard. "How many monkeys have I got in my pocket?"

None, thought Eddy. *It's obviously none.*

The Captain shouted back, "You have sev— No, wait a minute – you have fi—"

Say none!!! Eddy tried to push the thought out of his brain and into the Captain's. *Where could he have got a monkey from?*

"Let me work it out. Ummm – fou…no…"

Zero! Nought! Nil! Eddy yelled silently.

"Errrr… You have NO monkeys in your pocket," said the Captain.

At last, thought Eddy, *you've got the hang of this stupid game.*

"Bah!" shouted Barracuda Bill. "Correct!"

It was the Captain's turn to ask. "How many monkeys have I got in my pocket?"

Almost before the question ended, Barracuda Bill shouted back, "You have no monkeys in your pocket!"

"Round two!" cried a voice in the crowd.

"Wait!" said the Captain. "You're wrong."

"Whaaaaaaaaaaaaaaat?!"

The entire crowd gasped. They gasped so hard that the breeze nearly sucked Barracuda Bill's hat off his head, and his parrot had to dig its claws into his shoulder to hang on.

"I have one monkey in my pocket."

And now everyone was silent.

Barracuda Bill tugged the parrot out of his shoulder, and spat out the ritual reply: "Show me the monkey!"

35

SMALL MAN, BIG BOOK

The Captain reached into his pocket and pulled out a grubby blue and white spotted handkerchief. He laid it on the palm of his hand and gently unfolded it – and there, blinking in the sunlight, was a tiny monkey.

"Game to me," said the Captain triumphantly.

"Ouch!" he continued, as the monkey bit his finger, then ran up his arm, knocked his hat off, and leaped into the crowd. It scampered across their heads and away over the palace wall.

"We have a winner!" Not Important announced from the balcony. "Let riders be despatched to the furthest corners of the kingdom, to tell the people that the long search is over. Beautiful Princess Ermintrelda will marry Captain McHake!"

"My turn at last!" shouted Beautiful Princess Ermintrelda.

"You won, Captain!" said Eddy. "But where did you get that monkey from?"

"It was by the beach when I was looking for a path through the palm trees. He jumped out of a bush and snuggled onto my hand – cheeky little fellow. Well, you know the old proverb, 'A fool and his monkey are soon parted.' I was trying very hard not to be a fool, so I knew we shouldn't be parted, and I popped him in my pocket."

"And how did you work out that Barracuda Bill had no monkey? You never got that right before."

"Ah," said the Captain. "That's the arithmeticals for

you, ain't it? I knew that the chance of either one of us having a monkey was quite unlikely. But I also knew that I did have a monkey. And that was very unlikely. So the chance of Barracuda Bill also having a monkey must be about seven hundred and forty-three times more unlikely. And you don't have to be a genius to know that quite unlikely multiplied by very unlikely multiplied by seven hundred and forty-three equals downright impossible."

"I don't think it actually works like that," said Eddy, "but I'm very glad that you do."

"Like I said, I ain't no fool." He tapped his finger on the side of his nose and winked.

"So that was your plan," said the Crew. "I always knew you could do it."

"Me too," said the Penguin. "Almost."

"And soon we'll get our hands on all that lovely treasure," said the Captain. "It's a shame I'll have to marry the Princess as well, but we're going to be rich."

"Do you think Barracuda Bill is just going to let that happen?" said Eddy, suddenly realizing that they might have a problem. "This could be very dangerous – he and his crew might attack us at any moment."

But Barracuda Bill didn't look like he was about to attack. He was sitting on the ground, his shoulders sagging, his face drooping, a picture of unhappiness.

"But I love her," he muttered. "What am I going to do without her?"

His crew shuffled around looking embarrassed. Some of them started to edge away.

His parrot rubbed its head against his cheek.

"Poor old Bill," it said. "Boo-hoo."

Then it pooed down the back of his coat again.

"Come on, Skipper," said Jellyfish Jones, "I know how to cheer you up. Let's go and hit something until it breaks."

"Not in the mood," said Barracuda Bill. His bottom lip began to wobble.

"I don't think we need to worry about him right now," said the Captain. "All we have to do is claim the prize."

"He's right," said the Penguin. "Even I don't see how anything could go wrong this time."

"There is an objection!" It was Not Important's voice. "Let another lot of riders be despatched to catch up with the riders who have already left and tell them to hang on a bit and not say anything to anyone while we get this sorted out!"

"I don't believe it," said the Penguin. "Me and my big beak."

A short, bald man stepped forward onto the balcony.

"My name is Engelbert Gangplaster," he addressed the crowd. "I am the Palace Librarian and this" – he raised an enormous leather-bound book – "is an ancient and original copy of YE TRUE AND ONLIE RULYES OF YE SPORT OF WHAT SAY'ST THOU, FELLOW, IS THE QUANTITY OF MONKEYS THAT IN MY POCKET DO DWELL? I refer to page 217 – section twenty-six, paragraph xiv, subsection J, item 11b."

So that cheating and malpractice may not stain this noble sport, it is decreed that at contest end each player shall bring forth any monkey that he has played. And he shall offer his monkey for general inspection, to prove that it truly be a monkey, and neither a dog in disguise nor a peculiarly hairy infant child. Should ye player fail to present said monkey, let him be known to all for a sneaky scoundrel and suffer disqualification.

He closed the book with a thud, and pointed at the Captain. "Oi! You! Where's your monkey?"

"It ran off," said the Captain. "You all saw it go."

There was a muttering from *The Scavenger*'s crew.

"Looked like a dog in disguise to me," one voice broke out.

"Whippet in a wig," agreed a second. "I knew the moment I set eyes on it."

"Rubbish!" shouted Eddy.

"Hairy baby if ever I saw one," said another voice.

"The spitting image of my sister's youngest," added a fourth. "Scoundrel!"

"Cheat!" *The Scavenger*'s crew raised a racket. "Boo!"

"You all know it was a monkey!" shouted Eddy.

"Monkey or no monkey," Gangplaster bellowed from the balcony, "if you can't produce it for inspection, the book says you're out!"

"Oh, dear." Barracuda Bill was suddenly looking much more cheerful. "It seems you've been disqualificated."

"But I won," said the Captain. "Fair and square."

"Rules is rules," said Barracuda Bill.

"You said you hate rules," said Eddy.

"Not when they are on my side."

"I'm sorry, Captain dearie, but I don't see how we can argue with the official rule book." The Crew put an arm round the Captain's shoulder. "Not to mention the hundred hairy brutes on Bill's side."

"Which means no treasure," said the Captain sadly. "I'm sorry, Eddy – I've let you down again."

"No," said Eddy. "You haven't let me down. Don't get me wrong – I really wish we had won the treasure to save my gran's cottage. But I've realized that there's something more important than that. You proved how brave you are. You showed your real character. And I'm proud to call you Captain. And my friend."

"He's right," the Crew agreed. "That's worth more than gold."

"Not when you want to go shopping," said the Penguin.

"And look on the bright side," the Crew continued. "You didn't get horribly killed and you don't have to marry the Princess."

"Now that has cheered me up," said the Captain. "There's a great big sea out there and somewhere we'll find another way to get rich."

"We have a different winner!" announced Not Important. "Let even more riders be despatched to tell the first lot to rub out Captain McHake's name and put Barracuda Bill instead. Oh, and to tell the second lot they can come back home. The long search is over again. Beautiful Princess Ermintrelda will marry Barracuda Bill!"

"Is that definite this time?" asked Beautiful Princess Ermintrelda.

"Definitely definite," said Not Important.

"Oh, goody!" said the Princess. "I like him more than the other one. He's bigger and beardier. And he doesn't smell so much like a fish."

GETTING IT RIGHT BY GETTING IT WRONG

That night there was a mighty feast to celebrate the wedding, and the two ships' companies put their differences aside. The crew of *The Scavenger* drank a lot of beer and wine and rum and cider and port and gin and brandy and sherry, and when that had all gone one of them remembered a big bottle of something yellow and sweet and syrupy that he had brought back from his holidays and they drank that too.

Then there was singing and music and wild whirling dancing and sitting down feeling dizzy and a bit sick and saying that they knew it was a mistake to drink that sweet syrupy yellow stuff.

Jellyfish Jones made a speech about some of the hilariously stupid things that Barracuda Bill had got up to when he was young. Everybody laughed a lot because they really were completely hilarious and extraordinarily stupid.

Then Barracuda Bill made a speech about how he was the happiest man alive and if anyone ever repeated any of the things Jellyfish Jones had just told them, he would feed them to the goldfish because being eaten by sharks would be too quick and easy for them.

Then Beautiful Princess Ermintrelda made a speech about how this was the best day of her life. She knew the Captain must be dreadfully disappointed that she couldn't marry him too so that he could be the equal happiest man alive. She wanted to thank the Captain, because without him Barracuda Bill would have had no one to steal all her presents from. So before she handed all her vast store of treasure over to her new husband she thought the Captain should go and help himself to whatever gold and jewels he wanted.

And then the Captain didn't make a speech he just went to find a wheelbarrow.

♆ ♆ ♆

The next morning *The Scavenger*'s crew slept late and woke up with terrible headaches and declared that the sweet syrupy yellow stuff was the devil's own drink. Then they discovered that the Codcakers had already taken their wheelbarrow full of treasure down to their ship and sailed away.

Out at sea, the waves were calm. A breeze hurried a few scuffs of white cloud through a blue sky. The same breeze billowed *The Codcake*'s sails as it pushed the ship through the water. The magic map now showed a single word – HOME – with an arrow that pointed off its western edge.

On deck, Eddy and the Captain were examining the contents of the wheelbarrow. The Crew stood nearby at the ship's wheel. The Penguin was trying on a particularly fetching diamond and sapphire tiara with matching earrings and admiring himself in a mirror. All was well with the world.

"See anything you like?" asked the Captain. "Pick out something pretty for when we divides this lot up between us."

"I don't know where to start," said Eddy, turning the treasure over in his hands. "Necklaces and goblets and brooches and – hey – there's a ruby ring here, a bit like the one that we found in—"

His voice tailed off.

"Summat wrong?" asked the Captain.

"No," said Eddy. "Nothing's wrong. Look at this."

He held up a heavy gold band, set with a chunky ruby. The jewel had a skull etched into it. And in its right eye socket there was a tiny letter G.

"Grungeybeard," said the Captain in a low whisper. "Well I'll be—"

"It's part of Grungeybeard's treasure," said Eddy. "It really is. But how do you think it ended up at Ermintrelda's palace?"

"Who knows?" said the Captain. "Treasure's a restless thing. Give it a chance and it will wander. Which is why we are going to look after this little lot very carefully."

Eddy dug down into the wheelbarrow.

"There's a pearl down here that's as big as a conker, and a diamond the size of a gull's egg, and I've never seen a hamster that's as fat as this emerald. Just like in the legend of Grungeybeard's loot. You were right all along – even when you were wrong about the gingerbread. We found it."

"I never doubted it," said the Captain. "Well, yes I

did. But I was right in the end, wasn't I?"

"And you're not the only one," said the Crew.

"What do you mean?" said Eddy.

"Why did you say your parents had sent you to stay with your gran?"

"For fresh air and fun," said Eddy.

"Well, there's fresh air all around us now. And you're not going to tell me you haven't had fun."

"No," said Eddy. "This quest has been the most fun I've had in my life."

"So I would say that your parents got it right as well – even when they got it wrong. What do you think?"

"I think I miss them," said Eddy.

He gazed out over the water. *The Codcake* sliced through the sea, taking them home. The sound of the waves slapping against her hull mingled with the cries of the seabirds that wheeled overhead, and the faint, regular BOOM BOOM from far off over the...

BOOM BOOM?

BOOM
BOOM

277

The Scavenger was out there somewhere.

Eddy grabbed a telescope. And there she was, coming up behind them on the starboard side. Eddy knew she was faster than *The Codcake*. What would happen when she caught up? On the one hand, the two crews had feasted together like old friends. On the other hand, *The Scavenger* was manned by ruthless pirates, and *The Codcake* had a wheelbarrow full of treasure on her deck.

"Captain! It's *The Scavenger*!"

"Perhaps they just want to say goodbye," said the Crew, "after that lovely party."

"Or perhaps," said the Penguin, "they want to steal the treasure, feed us to the sharks and blow up the ship."

"I just don't know," said the Captain. "And we'll only find out when they catch us."

"So we'd better be prepared," said Eddy. "You stood up to Barracuda Bill, Captain. I think it's time for *The Codcake* to stand up to *The Scavenger*. If they are coming for the treasure, we're not going to give it to them without a fight. This time, we're going to be ready for them."

THE MORNING AFTER THE NIGHT BEFORE

"Us? Ready? Really?" asked the Captain.

"We'll all have to work together as fast as we can," said Eddy. "We need to drag every heavy object we can find out of the hold. We're going to tie long ropes on them and hang them from the starboard yards—"

"The whats?" asked the Crew.

"The yards – the long bits of wood that the sails hang down from. Then we need to haul the heavy things up the mainmast and lash them tight. We'll need a block and tackle for that."

"There's one in the rucksack, dearie."

"And then—"

"Hold hard!" said the Captain. "Remember who gives the orders round here. Right, everybody, you've got to block the hall with yards of rope, then tackle your lashes and…oh, stinky fish! Do what Eddy just said! And be quick about it!"

After an hour of huffing and heaving and hauling, the job was done. Dozens of ropes were tied along the starboard yards, their other ends attached to half the contents of *The Codcake*'s hold – saucepans and sea boots and buckets and enough assorted ironmongery to open a shop, all lashed to the mainmast with a single long cord that was knotted off down by the deck.

Eddy looked up and smiled.

"And that," he said, "is our plan."

"First rate!" said the Captain. "Remind me, what was it again?"

"You'll see," said Eddy. "Crew, stand by the mast. When I give the signal, untie that big knot."

"Right," said the Crew, taking hold of the loose end of the cord.

BOOM
BOOM

The Scavenger was closing fast. Eddy noticed that the booming stamping noise wasn't nearly as loud as usual.

"Where we going?"

And the chanting was almost a whisper.

"What we doing?"

A hundred voices hissed.

"Are we there yet?"

The Scavenger drew up to *The Codcake's* starboard side. The pirates were gathered on deck, with Jellyfish Jones at their head, and no sign of Barracuda Bill.

"Ahoy there!" the Captain yelled.

"Keep your voice down!" croaked Jellyfish. "We've a lot of sore heads on board. If I ever remember who brought that bottle of sweet syrupy yellow stuff, I'll make him suffer."

"Marvellous party, though."

"Party's over now. It's back to real life. Except for Barracuda Bill. The most twisted, devious and downright vicious headcase I've ever met – what a guy. You know what he was doing this morning? Sitting with his missus putting kittens into baskets. The world has turned upside down. Quite frankly, I'm in bits. Bits."

"Can we help you?" asked the Captain.

"Indeed you can," said Jellyfish. "Or we can come across and help ourselves. Either way, we want that treasure. And lads, remember, if you are chopping anyone into little pieces, do it very, very, quietly."

A hundred very grumpy pirates edged towards *The Codcake*, cutlasses at the ready.

"Now!" Eddy shouted to the Crew.

The Crew yanked on the cord, undoing the knot and releasing all the heavy objects that were lashed to the mast. They swung down on the ends of their ropes, arcing towards *The Scavenger*'s deck.

"Duck!" shouted Eddy.

"For the last time, I'm not a flipping duck!" the Penguin replied. "I'm a – oh, got you!" And he hit the deck as a tin bucket whistled past him.

The broadside of hardware was as effective as any cannon. The first saucepan hit a hairy pirate square on the chin and launched him backwards, flattening three shipmates standing behind him. Down the objects hurtled, dozen upon dozen of them, like flying fists of justice. And terrible was the judgement that they dealt. They caught the pirates completely by surprise, whooshing and swooping and knocking them flying.

Men, swords, pistols, hats and wooden legs went spinning across the deck.

The pirates tried to dodge out of the way, but they might as well have tried to run through a storm and avoid the raindrops.

Some were bashed
clean over the far side
of the ship, and
sent splashing and
cursing into the
sea. A few even chose
to jump overboard to
avoid the furious bombardment.
By the time the swinging
missiles slowed to a halt, the attack
had laid out every man on
The Scavenger.

Every man, that is, but one.
Jellyfish Jones rose from behind the
cannon, where he had taken cover, with
a scowl on his face and a cutlass in his hand. He leaped
across the gap between the two ships, landed on *The
Codcake*'s deck, and lunged towards the Captain.

The Captain reached for his own sword – and
realized with horror that he had left it on the big pile
of weapons in the courtyard at Ermintrelda's palace.
He scrabbled wildly for something –
anything – to defend himself.

His hand found the carrot on his shoulder.
He grabbed it and held it out in front of him like
a dagger.

The sight was so ridiculous that it halted
Jellyfish Jones's charge. He sneered at the
Captain with a snort of laughter.
"You have got to be joking."
That moment gave
Eddy time to react.

Jellyfish raised
his cutlass, ready
to strike.

Eddy launched himself at Jellyfish, catching him behind the knees with his full weight. Jellyfish's legs buckled and he pitched forward…

"Waaaah!"

…jabbing his right eye down hard on the end of the carrot.

"Owwwwwww!"

He instinctively raised his hand to his throbbing eye…

DONK!

…but he was still holding his cutlass. Its heavy metal handguard whacked into his forehead.

"Aaaarrrrgghh!"

He staggered dizzily back to *The Scavenger* and collapsed in a heap. "We surrender," he croaked.

"We did it!" Eddy yelled. The Codcakers broke into victorious cheers.

"And please stop shouting," Jellyfish moaned, clutching his aching head, as *The Scavenger* drifted away from *The Codcake*.

"Crew!" said the Captain. "Set a course for home."

"I wonder how long it will take," said Eddy.

"We won't get there at all," said the Crew, "unless we untie those ropes."

She was right. Now that all the heavy objects were hanging straight down from the starboard yards, their weight was making the ship lean alarmingly. One big wave across their bows would have them over.

Eddy climbed the mast, shinned out along the yards, and set about cutting them loose. It took him quite a while, but finally he sliced through the last rope, and the last object dropped onto the deck below. For the first time since he had started, he looked up – and there ahead, just a few miles away, was the familiar shape of Tidemark Bay.

"Land ahoy, Captain!" he shouted.

News of the sight of the strange ship travelled quickly round the little town. By the time *The Codcake* sailed into the harbour, what looked like the entire population of Tidemark Bay had gathered by the water's edge. *The Codcake* slowed as she came home, then nestled against the quayside as softly as a cat settling on a friendly lap.

Eddy lowered the gangplank, and found himself face-to-face with the two boys who had thrown tomatoes at him when he first set out. The bigger one stood weighing a half-rotten pineapple in his hand.

"Oi! Look what I've got for you," he sniggered, ready to hurl it.

"You know what?" said Eddy. "We've just battled a hundred hardened pirates, tangled with the maddest menace in all the ocean, seen off an evil sweet maker and escaped from being chained up in a dungeon. Oh, yes, and been this close to getting our heads bitten off by a huge smelly beast. So if that bit of fruit is the best you can do, bring it on."

He stared straight at the boy. The boy dropped his gaze, and shrugged.

"Not bothered," he mumbled. He tossed the pineapple into the waters of the harbour, and slouched away. "Come on," he grunted to his companion.

But the other boy didn't move.

"Nice boat," he said to Eddy. "Did you really almost get your head bitten off?"

"I'll tell you about it sometime," said Eddy. "But right now I've got to find someone."

His gran. He suddenly realized that she must have been worried sick wondering where he had gone.

How long had they been away? Four days? Five? She had probably called the police. They would have been out searching for him. He was going to be in big trouble.

He pushed through the crowd, trying to spot her. And there she was.

He ran over.

"Gran! I'm so sorry!"

The old lady looked puzzled.

"Hello, Eddy. Have you come to visit? That's nice."

She has forgotten I was here, Eddy thought. *She hasn't missed me at all.* He let out a huge sigh. There wasn't going to be any trouble.

"Yes," he said, "I've come to stay."

But he hadn't quite got away with it. His gran looked him up and down, and frowned.

"What on earth," she asked sternly, "have you done with your socks?"

⚓ ⚓ ⚓

That summer was the busiest that Tidemark Bay had
seen for years. Word of *The Codcake* and its fabulous haul
brought tourists flocking. The owners of hotels and
boarding houses rooted in the backs of cupboards to find
their long-neglected *No Vacancies* signs. The fish and
chip shops took on extra staff. A thousand tents bloomed
in the hills above the harbour.

The Captain held court on board the ship. He got rid
of his hammock, and spent a tiny fraction of the
treasure on a very comfortable reclining armchair,
which he placed just outside his cabin door. And there
he would sit bouncing small children on his knee while
thrilling crowds of visitors with stories of *The Codcake's*
fantastic adventures – some of which were almost true.
Sometimes the children brought him storybooks to
read, and helped him out with the hard words. And
every night, he let off fireworks, which burst brightly
above the town in very satisfying explosions.

The Crew turned her shop into a museum where she
displayed some of the finest of the treasure, alongside
her unique collection of antiques and curios. Visitors
were especially amused by the copper jelly mould

shaped like an octopus and the stuffed lobster dressed as a soldier. She also ran a competition to guess what a strange old machine was used for. The winner said it was for peeling potatoes. The prize was the strange old machine, which the Crew was frankly glad to see the back of.

The Penguin built a smart new restaurant on the site where Captain Cockle had once sold his Crunchy Codcakes. Here he served the freshest fish on the coast, and entertained the diners with his act. He had lots of customers, because the fish was delicious. And although his jokes weren't very funny, and his dancing was quite clumsy, and you can live without hearing a selection of disco classics played on old-fashioned rubber car horns, everyone agreed that it's not every day that you get to see a penguin wearing a particularly fetching diamond and sapphire tiara with matching earrings.

Eddy gave his gran more than enough of the treasure to fix up her cottage. She spent the enough on the repairs, and used the more than to open a new amusement arcade. She went there every day to watch tourists feed money into the one-armed bandits. She was never going to be short of cash again. And as her worries disappeared, so did the scattiness that had fuddled her brain.

Eddy gave another share of his treasure to his parents. Now they could afford to leave their busy jobs in the city, move to Tidemark Bay, and open the little business they had always dreamed of. The little business they had always dreamed of turned out to be one that made superhero fancy-dress outfits for pets – but nobody's perfect.

Eddy spent the rest of the summer having a great time with his old friends from *The Codcake*, and his new friends from the town. All the local kids wanted to play with the boy who had sailed on a pirate ship, and had incredible adventures, and brought home amazing treasures. They didn't call him "Oi! Cityboy Snotface!" any more. Or just "Oi!" for short. They called him "Eddy" or "Eddy Stone". And sometimes, when they wanted to show off to people because he was their mate, they called him "*the* Eddy Stone".

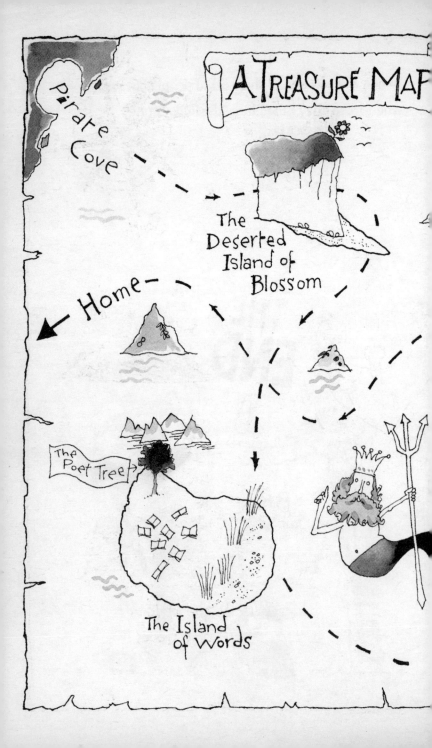

The Island of Fear
HERE BE MONSTERS
NORTH
West
East
South
Rocky Island
The Island of One Thousand and One Towers
PLOVERDEW'S
The Island of Rare and Exotic Goods

THE CAPTAIN'S
SEASICK SEA SHANTY

What shall we do with the seasick sailor
What shall we do with the seasick sailor
What shall we do with the seasick sailor
Early in the morning?

HUEY! And up it rises
GROOEY! And up it rises
SPEWEY! And up it rises
Early in the morning.

If he's feeling queasy and he needs to retch up
Feed him something greasy that he's sure to fetch up
Sausage, egg and bacon and a pint of ketchup
Early in the morning.

HUEY! And up it rises
GROOEY! And up it rises
SPEWEY! And up it rises
Early in the morning.

Empty out his tummy he'll appreciate it
Cook a sardine curry - he won't tolerate it
Wash it down with rum - and he'll regurgitate it
Early in the morning.

HUEY! And up it rises
GROOEY! And up it rises
SPEWEY! And up it rises
Early in the morning.

Slop seaweed stew and custard in a rusty bucket
Make him swallow <u>all</u> of that revolting muck. It
Won't take very long - then he'll be sure to chuck it
Early in the morning.

HUEY! And up it rises
GROOEY! And up it rises
SPEWEY! And up it rises
Early in the morning.

THE POET TREE'S
POEM FOR THE CAPTAIN

Oh! The pirate life is thrilling
And the lads are bold and gruff
They do pillaging and stealing
And other rough tough stuff.

But a pirate can get thinking
And a pirate can get glum
For there's more to life than fighting,
Treasure, yo ho ho and rum.

Nights grow lonely in my hammock
When the ocean wind blows cold
Like a ship without a cargo
I've got nothing in my hold.

I have heard the mermaids murmur
But a mermaid's half a fish
And I want a girl with legs and not
A scaly tail to swish.

I've sung soft songs to the waters
On my heartstrings tunes I've played
But there's no one in the seas except
Sardines to serenade.

From fair ladies I've been castaway
Adrift, alone, marooned.
But now Cupid's shot an arrow
And my heart has been harpooned.

It's with love for you he's struck me
With that missile from his quiver
You have set my boat a-floating
And made all my timbers shiver.

Love has left me feeling groggy
By my poem be enticed
Let my woozy wooing win you
Like the mainbrace, let's get spliced.

Let us knot our ropes together
I am useless on my own
Like a cannon with no powder
Like a skull with no crossbone.

Will you say you'll be my sweetheart?
Will you end my misery?
It's the tears of lonely sailors
That turn all the seas salty.

READ MORE AMAZING ADVENTURES FEATURING

By Simon Cherry
Illustrated by Francis Blake

"Wonderfully told adventures"
Stephen Fry

"Total silliness"
Lenny Henry

PRAISE FOR
EDDY STONE

"A cracker and very, very funny too." **LoveReading4Kids**

"A charming, surreal and batty trip into a world of…
buried treasure and total silliness. Lovely." **Lenny Henry**

"Highly entertaining and swashbuckling!" **Booktrust**

"Made me laugh out loud…a fantastically silly pirate
adventure." **Sarah McIntyre**

"The best adventure series you'll see on the high seas this
year!" **Lancashire Evening Post**

"Oh how I wish the wonderfully told adventures of this
unforgettable pirate and the boy who befriends him had
existed when I was young." **Stephen Fry**

"Ripping yarns." **The Big Issue**

"This book [*Eddy Stone and the Epic Holiday Adventure*] was
shortlisted for the Laugh Out Loud awards. Because it
made us laugh out loud." **Nicolette Jones, Sunday Times
Children's Books Editor and Lollies judge**

ABOUT THE AUTHOR

Before he started writing children's books, Simon Cherry spent almost twenty years making television documentaries in the Arts Department at ITV. He has also written for newspapers, magazines and the stage. Simon lives in Surrey with his wife, two teenage sons, and a ginger cat who is in charge of everyone else. When not writing, he spends a lot of time looking at the garden and wishing it would weed itself. So far, this has not worked.

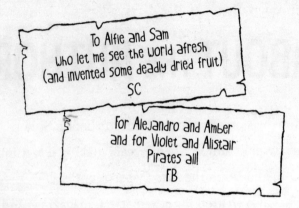

To Alfie and Sam
who let me see the world afresh
(and invented some deadly dried fruit)
SC

For Alejandro and Amber
and for Violet and Alistair
Pirates all!
FB

This edition published 2018. First published in the UK in 2016 as "Eddy Stone and the Epic Holiday Mash-up" by Usborne Publishing Ltd., Usborne House, 83-85 Saffron Hill, London EC1N 8RT, England. www.usborne.com

Text copyright © Simon Cherry, 2016
The right of Simon Cherry to be identified as the author of this work has been asserted by him in accordance with the Copyright, Designs and Patents Act, 1988.

Illustrations copyright © Usborne Publishing Ltd., 2016
Illustrations by Francis Blake.

The name Usborne and the devices ♀ 🎈 are Trade Marks of Usborne Publishing Ltd.

A CIP catalogue record for this book is available from the British Library.

JFMA JJASOND /18

ISBN 9781474953771 03900/5
Printed in the UK.